PICTURES
OF THE
NIGHT

RED FOX DEFiNiTiONS

PICTURES
OF THE
NIGHT

ADÈLE GERAS

RED FOX DEFiniTiOnS

World's End

'ONCE upon a time,' I said, 'I had a mother, but I killed her.'

Greg said, 'You're being melodramatic as usual, Bella. Try and get a little rest. What happened yesterday has made you think along these morbid lines, that's what it is. I don't believe you killed your mother at all.'

'She died when I was born though.'

'That's not the same thing, is it? You didn't mean to kill her. The intention wasn't there, so the whole affair becomes sad, of course, but not exactly lurid.'

'You're as bad as Megan and Alice,' I sighed. 'They're forever telling me off for exaggerating, making an exhibition of myself, being what you call melodramatic.'

Greg strummed a few notes on his guitar. He was sitting on the end of the bed, looking after me. Because of what happened yesterday, I'd been put in the best bed in the whole house, the one in Pete's room. All the others were out for some reason or other. Greg's fair hair flopped over on to his forehead, almost hiding his eyes. He looked cuddly, in spite of being over six feet tall. He'd folded his legs into strange shapes, to squeeze on to the small amount of space left over on the bed after I'd stretched my legs out as far as they would go.

'Who is Megan . . . What is she . . .' he sang, to the tune of 'Who is Sylvia?', and I kicked him through the blankets. He stopped singing and added, 'and Alice too, if it comes to that.'

'I keep telling you and you never listen,' I said. 'It's because you've always got your nose in a guitar. Megan and Alice are my friends at school, at Egerton Hall.'

'Oh, very la-di-da, I'm sure!'

'Shut up and pay attention. They are my best friends. We used to share a room called the Tower Room, but then last Easter term Megan ran away to London with Simon, the rather sweet laboratory assistant . . .'

'Did you report the story to the *News of the World*? You could have made a bit of money.'

'Greg, belt up! I'm telling you something. Megan came back to do her A-level exams. Can you imagine? Leaving the one you love and coming back to school? I can't. Simon went off to America in a huff.'

'When I go to America,' said Greg, 'I shall try and go in a plane. They're more reliable than huffs.'

'I give up.' I pulled the blankets over my head and pretended to be hurt. 'You're not a bit interested, so I'll keep quiet.'

'No, Bella, truly, I'm sorry.' Greg jumped off the foot of the bed and came to find my face under the covers. He looked very contrite. I said:

'If you interrupt me again, I'll never say another word to you. Not ever.'

As soon as I'd said it, I regretted it. Greg looked stricken, so I laughed.

'I don't mean it, Greg, only you're an impossible person to tell a story to. Just sit still and listen.'

And Greg did listen, because I told him about Alice, and about how she was raped on the night of her eighteenth birthday party, just a couple of weeks ago. That silenced him for a bit, then he said:

'Where is she now?'

'In her bedroom. She won't speak to anyone. She won't see anyone. Megan and I have just been told to wait till she gets better.'

'You could write letters,' Greg suggested.

'I have, but there's no point in sending them. She wouldn't be able to read them. Poor Alice!' I hated to think of her, in her room in Arcadia House. What if she wasn't really in a coma, as we'd been told? What if she knew what was happening and just thought Megan and I had stopped caring about her? I couldn't bear that, and so every now and then I would write to her, and put the letter in my suitcase. I felt sure she'd be herself one day, because I simply couldn't face any other possibility and I was keeping all the letters to show her I'd been thinking about her.

'I don't know,' said Greg. 'It's not a bit what I'd imagined went on in a girls' school. Running off to London with your lover isn't exactly school story stuff, and as for your other friend . . .' Greg looked at me. 'I don't know what to say. You must feel . . .' He couldn't find the right words and I couldn't help him. I closed my eyes.

What happened yesterday was very strange, or was I really being melodramatic? I don't care. Long live melodrama, say I, and passion and bright scarlet dresses and loud music and everything that isn't flat and dull and grey and little and ordinary. I hate ordinary things, and ordinary people bore me to death.

There's nothing ordinary about Pete and the band. I met them at a party in December 1961, which was only last year though it seems ages ago now. The party was at the Establishment Club which was *the* place to go, and that very evening they had taken me to another nightclub, where I sang with them for the very first time. Since then they've let me perform with the band now and again, whenever I could, and once or twice when I couldn't. Last February, I sneaked out of Egerton Hall to sing at a Valentine's Day ball and climbed back into the Tower Room up the same scaffolding that Megan's Simon used in order to reach her. Last holidays, I visited Pete's house a couple of times, but now I'm staying here. After what happened to Alice, I can't really face going home. The advantage of having a fantastically busy father and a stepmother who permanently wishes you as far as possible from where she is, is that you can stay away from home for ages. I haven't told them exactly where I am. They think I'm staying with an aunt of Alice's. Alice has thirteen aunts who are useful in all sorts of ways, and providing an alibi for me is what they're doing now. I write a postcard home every few days and phone occasionally, but Marjorie, my wicked stepmother, is so relieved to be rid of me that she'll accept any story I tell her. My father thinks Marjorie has the whole situation under control, and so he's happy too. It's an ideal arrangement.

I looked at Greg. He was deeply into a song he'd been working on for some days. There were scrappy pieces of paper all over the floor, and a pencil that had seen better days and had totally forgotten what a sharpener looked like, and Greg had slipped off the bed and taken up residence amidst all the chaos on the floor. From time to time he'd play a few notes on the guitar, and these little snippets of melody would hang in the silence for a few moments, and then disappear. I knew Greg would now be unreachable until he'd finished whatever it was he was writing, so I decided to think quietly back over everything that had happened since I'd come to Pete's house, here in this part of London where Chelsea ceases to be Chelsea and becomes World's End.

I like the name: World's End. It has a certain ring of doom to it, you've got to admit. In fact, the street is full of stuccoed houses fallen on hard times. Pete's house is tall and thin. I liked it from the very first time I saw it because it was the exact opposite of my house, and could have been specifically designed as Marjorie's idea of Hell.

There were three floors full of rooms, each one more cluttered and messy than the last. It reminded me of a doll's house, because all sorts of strange objects (a large stuffed bear, a tiger-skin rug, brass trays on gate-leg tables, the odd dragon-shaped kite, a marble urn, the propeller from an ancient aircraft) were dotted about all over the place, as though some giant child had been playing and left them lying about for the dolls to wonder at. As well as peculiar bits and pieces everywhere, there was all the mess you'd expect from seven men living together. That was how I'd expressed it to Megan, when I told her about it last term.

'I don't see any reason why men shouldn't be as tidy as women, do you?' she'd said.

'No,' I said. 'There isn't any reason, but this lot are amazing. I tease them about it. I say things like: "Didn't your mother ever tell you dirty socks go in a laundry basket?" and they just laugh and say: "What's a laundry basket?" Dave, whose mother died when he was quite young, says: "You can come and look after us. Teach us how to take care of ourselves," and Pete laughs and says: "Better yet, come and take care of us yourself!"'

'I can't believe you will,' Megan had smiled. 'You're not what I'd call the house-proud type.'

'I'm not, it's true, but honestly, Megan, in that house it's tidy it up yourself or risk vanishing altogether in a rising ride of garbage.'

Now that I'm staying here, I do try and make things as pleasant as possible. Megan and Alice would be astonished, but I enjoy the gratitude I get from Pete and the others. They are all so delighted with everything. Even quite a simple idea like gathering up all the waste paper no one wants off the floor and putting it into the dustbin was greeted like a major discovery the first time I did it, and really daring initiatives like running some hot water into a basin and washing a few dishes, well, I felt as though I'd just topped the bill at the London Palladium, I got so much praise.

I had the nicest room in the house, somewhere all to myself. That was an accident. The first time I ever found this house, no one was in. This didn't matter as it turned out, because the front door wasn't locked. Later, I discovered that it frequently remained open, because the stiff mortise lock needed oiling, and the old-fashioned keys were always getting themselves mislaid. It was the middle of the afternoon when I turned up, and the place was deserted. I knew the address, of course, but I'd come on the off-chance that they'd be in, and could give me a cup of tea. I'd been shopping in the King's Road, and felt quite worn out. I snooped around a bit, but only on the ground floor, and eventually found myself in a small room at the back of the house. There was a battered old chaise-longue in there, upholstered in moth-eaten puce velvet with sad-looking braid in a tarnished gold colour clinging here and there to the wreckage. I can remember thinking: I'll just lie down here for a moment and think what to do next, and then I suppose I must have fallen asleep.

When I woke up, hours later, darkness had fallen, and Pete and the boys were all standing round and looking at me. Waking up and finding them, all seven of them, staring at me while I slept was a bit of a shock, but I pulled myself together and sat up. They still looked quite alarming, all shadowy and enormous. Later on, I realized that this must have been because of the unusual lighting arrangements in the house. Pete hated any kind of fixture dangling from the ceiling and abhorred what he called 'chilly light' and the rooms were full of light bulbs in shades of red and yellow screwed into the tops of bottles that had been turned into lamps and then quite deliberately hidden behind other pieces of furniture. This meant that you could never see where the light was coming from and wherever it fell it cast long, medieval-looking shadows on the walls and ceilings. Reading in bed was out of the question, although Pete did have a supply of candles and cracked saucers. You could actually do it: take a candle and go upstairs from the kitchen singing, 'Here comes a candle to light you to bed'.

'But,' said Pete on the first night, 'I wouldn't recommend it. I reckon it's a fire hazard. Anyone still lively enough to want to read in bed can stay and do it in the kitchen. There's a decent-enough light in there.'

Of course, we never were lively enough. The music sessions went on till late in the orange dimness of the lounge or in Pete's room, where the darkness loomed in the corners and the shadows of the instruments danced along the walls.

That was after I had become a member of the household. On the first night, though, they led me down to the kitchen which was in the basement. Over coffee, I asked them if I could stay for a bit. They all said I could and seemed to take it for granted that the old chaise-longue was to be my bed, so that little room became mine, complete with a rocking chair with the seat missing, a couple of traffic signals, the odd car number-plate, two crash helmets and a drum kit.

'What about a cupboard?' I could imagine Megan asking. 'Isn't there a cupboard or a chest of drawers?' There isn't of course, but one can manage very well with open suitcases and garments draped over the back of the rocking chair. You never know what you can do till you try, as Marjorie has never tired of telling me.

Megan and Alice could never get the individual members of the band quite straight in their heads.

'You're not trying,' I used to say. 'Megan, you managed Alice's thirteen aunts quite well. I can't think why seven men is so difficult for you.'

There's Pete and Dave and Phil and Steve and Kenny and Harry and Greg. Pete's the leader of the band. He's thin and bearded and dark, and looks like a benevolent pirate. Harry's everyone's darling. Easygoing. Affable. Happy-go-lucky, with a round face and twinkling blue eyes.

'Girls love him,' I used to tell Megan and Alice. 'He sits there behind his drums and grins at them and they cluster around him afterwards wanting kisses and autographs.'

'And does Harry oblige?' Megan had wanted to know, and I knew what she was really asking.

'He's not my type,' I told her, 'but it would be very hard not to like him.'

They were all of them kind to me, and looked after me, but Greg . . . Greg loves me. I know that, although he hasn't actually said anything. Greg's eyes when he looks at me are full of devotion, and he's the one, who, from the first, spent every possible moment with me, always sat next to me at meals and took me about with him all over the place. Perhaps it's because he's the youngest member of the band, and only three years older than me. He has written songs for me to sing, he says, and he will show them to me soon.

It was Greg who took me to Jeannie's shop for the very first time. I suppose most people would call 'Aladdin's Cave' a junk shop, but it was full of treasures: old silk scarves and pieces of lace and jewellery and feathers and buttons and cushions in velvet covers and old uniforms and cracked records. I loved it from the moment I stepped into it, and I liked Jeannie, the owner, immediately. She is one of those amazingly glamorous slatterns with a face ravaged by time and alcohol and teeth practically ochre-coloured from too many cigarettes, but still tremendously vivid, alive. She has huge brown eyes, wears lashings of rouge and never puts anything on her body that you can actually identify as a proper garment, like a skirt or a cardigan or a pair of trousers. Jeannie just seems to be wrapped, or enveloped, in all sorts of pieces of fabric that are pinned or tied or held together somehow in an arrangement that manages to look exotic: strange and beautiful. All the floaty bits are always such colours: pinks and tangerines and saffron yellows and mossy greens and always, somewhere, different textures and surfaces of black: velvet, satin, chiffon or wool. Oh, I thought when I first saw her, she's like a sort of magic butterfly. That was one side of her character. The other was very practical. She always, for instance, wore slippers or gym shoes, saying that winklepickers were as bad for you in their way as binding up the feet in the old Chinese style. And she smelled extraordinary. I'm very knowledgeable about perfume, but these smells that hung about her shop were new to me.

'Oils,' she told me. 'Oriental oils. Patchouli, Bergamot and Sandalwood.'

She burned fragrant joss sticks in the shop so that the very air smelled magical. And she had a sense of humour, too. She told me her real name wasn't Jeannie at all.

'But,' she said, 'how can you have an Aladdin's cave and no genie? I changed it, that's all. Changed it to fit the shop. I ran a sea-food restaurant once. Down in Brighton, that was, called "Full Fathom Five" and guess what I was called?'

I couldn't guess. I suggested silly things like 'Shrimp' and 'Squid' but she waved her garments at me.

'Give over, Bella! You're not trying, are ya? I called myself Pearl then, didn't I? See?'

'Sea? North Sea? Irish Sea? Which sea do you mean?' I said and Jeannie shook with laughter.

'Ooh, Bella,' she shrieked. 'You are a caution and no mistake.'

I used to go to Aladdin's Cave almost every day, partly to see Jeannie and partly because there were always new goodies to be found there, especially in the boxes set out on trestle tables on the pavement outside the shop, where nothing cost more than a shilling. Greg usually came with me, but yesterday I was alone in the house.

'I don't like leaving you all on your own here,' Greg said. 'You be sure and lock the door now and don't open it to just anyone.'

'I don't know what you think's going to happen to me,' I said. 'No one even knows I'm here. Anyway, I thought I'd go down to Jeannie's shop for a while.'

'Don't be long then,' Greg said. 'And make sure you lock the door behind you when you get back.'

'You sound like my dad,' I told him. 'I'll be fine.'

And I was fine. I set out for Aladdin's Cave feeling very cheerful, and began rummaging happily through the shilling boxes as soon as I'd said hello to Jeannie.

I didn't really pay much attention to the woman who passed close beside me to go into the shop. I only noticed, in a half-hearted, absent-minded sort of way, that she smelt very faintly of 'Je Reviens' and that as she passed, a cloud spread itself over the sun and I felt, all at once, quite cold. She was inside the shop with Jeannie for about fifteen minutes and then she left. I got a better look at her this time. What struck me about her was that she appeared faded, as though she were a faint carbon copy of a real person. She wore grey and her hair was grey and she had most of her face hidden in a chiffon scarf. She was carrying a battered brown suitcase, and she walked quickly past me, and down the road. At the time, I could have sworn she didn't even look at me.

'Who's that?' I asked Jeannie.

'One of my suppliers,' Jeannie said. 'No one you'd be interested in. She brings me bits of lace and stuff.'

When I went home, I let myself in with my key, and slammed the door behind me. I forgot to lock it, of course. We all forgot, all the time, and no one ever troubled us. It wasn't as though there was anything worth stealing in the house. I went down to the kitchen to make some tea. I hadn't been there more than five minutes, when I heard someone in the hall.

'Hell-oo,' said an unfamiliar voice. 'Yoo-hoo! Is there anyone at home?'

It was a woman, and she was calling out to me, so I didn't feel at all nervous. She must be a neighbour, I thought, one I haven't met yet. I'd better go and see what she wants.

I walked up to the hall, and the first thing I saw was a white cat. It looked just like Snowflake, the cat I used to have when I was very young, the cat that my stepmother had claimed she was allergic to . . . I didn't want to be remind-ed of her, and I wanted this one out of the house. I said:

'Is that your cat?' to the woman who was standing in the shadows by the hatstand, and then I saw she was the one from Jeannie's shop. She even had her brown suitcase at her feet. I looked at the pretty, fluffy creature who by this time had run up a few stairs and was sitting there as though it intended to stay. I said, 'How did you know where I live? Did you follow me? And is that your cat?'

'That's no cat of mine, ducky. I'm what you might call

allergic to them. Must have crept in behind me . . . and yes, dear, I did follow you, cos I saw you at Jeannie's, didn't I, and I says to meself, Em, old girl, that child's a real beauty and if ever you had an ideal customer, she's the one.' The woman took a step forward and patted her suitcase. 'I've got stuff in here, dearie, that'll make your heart beat faster, and that's why I came after you, see? To show you . . .'

'Why didn't you show this stuff to me, whatever it is, when you noticed me in the shop? I don't like the thought of you following me, I must say.'

'Well, I'm very sorry, I'm sure, miss, but I meant no harm, honest. Only you've got to be a bit smart in my line of work, see. Seize any opportunity that comes along, like. And you being such a pretty girl, I thought: she'll love you for this, Em. She won't be able to resist what you've got to show her.' She patted the brown suitcase encouragingly and smiled.

I have to admit that I was tempted. There seemed to be no actual harm in her, although something in her manner, or her way of smiling, sent a shiver down my spine.

'Well, come in then,' I said reluctantly. 'Come down to the kitchen. I was just making some tea.'

'Oh,' said the woman (Em, she'd called herself). 'I can see that I was right about you, sure enough. Not only beautiful, but kind.'

She pulled a chair up to the table and sat down with her brown suitcase beside her. 'Two sugars, if you don't mind.'

I made the tea. The cat (oh, he did look like Snowflake! Who did he belong to? He wasn't one of the cats I'd seen wandering in the back gardens. I must ask Greg about him) came into the kitchen and jumped on to the windowsill.

All the time we were drinking our tea, the woman babbled on. I felt more and more uncomfortable, because what she was talking about was me, and my looks. She seemed to be gloating over them, but underneath the praise, the compliments, the extravagant comparisons she kept making between me and every famous beauty you can imagine, I could feel – this is the best way I have of describing it – a thick layer of dislike, of envy and even malice in everything she said. Clouds had massed in the sky and it was getting quite dark in the kitchen. I wanted to go and turn the light on, but to do this, I'd have had to pass Em's chair and this made me hesitate. Suddenly I wanted her gone: out of the house. Something in the way she drank her tea, the way she sat at the table was very familiar. I could hardly see her face in the dim light. I said:

'All my friends will be back in a minute. Don't you think you'd better show me what you've got in your case? That is, after all, why you came, isn't it?'

She stood up. 'It is! Of course it is!' she said. 'May I put my case here on the table?'

'Yes,' I said, 'and could you turn the light on, too, please? The switch is on the wall over there.'

She was obviously cleverer than I realized. She was quite right about the contents of her case. It had in it everything in the world that I most desired: exquisitely beautiful scarves and shawls and fans and jewels. I wanted every single thing. I said:

'You're right. It's all very beautiful, but I can't afford any of this. I haven't got much money.'

'Then let me make you a small present,' she said. 'After all, you did invite me in for tea.' She laughed and I thought: I've heard that laugh before somewhere, and then the thought left my head like a trail of smoke floating away from a cigarette.

'Oh, no, I couldn't,' I said. 'I couldn't accept a present.'

'I don't see why not,' she said, 'if it pleases me to give you one.' She pulled a wide pink suede belt from the whirlpool of laces and silks that frothed in her case and said:

'Come over here and let's try this for size.'

I went and stood in front of her. I was mesmerized, fascinated to see how I would look. I was wearing black trousers and a black polo-necked jumper. I stood in front of Em and raised my arms so that she could put the belt around my waist and tie the thongs of fine leather that held the ends together at the back. It seemed to take her rather a long time.

'It's a bit fiddly,' she said, 'this fastening. Good job I'm here to help you, eh?'

'Yes,' I said. 'Thank you very much.'

'Don't thank me, duck. It's made for you, that belt. There's no one else would suit it like you do.'

She left soon after that, and I was glad to close the door on her. I flew upstairs after she'd gone and stood in front of the only mirror in the house (propped up beside the window in Pete's room) to admire myself. I looked wonderful, and went to the window to see if I could still see Em in the road. There she was, down by the corner, gazing up at me. The thought came to me: that could be Marjorie . . . that's how she walks exactly. Well, I told myself, there's nothing strange about that. People often do resemble one another. I pranced about in front of the mirror for a while, enjoying how tiny my waist looked in my new belt. Then I thought: I'd better take it off, and I pulled it round so that the fastening was now at the front where I could undo it. It was laced up like a shoe, and I began pulling at the ends of the laces, thinking that the knot would fall open at once, but it didn't, and the harder I pulled the tighter the belt became and the angrier I felt. I'd seen a special chair in a museum once, long ago, into which they tied criminals, binding them to the back and arms by an intricate arrangement of leather straps. The more the prisoner struggled, the tighter the bonds grew, until they cut cruelly into flesh. This belt was like that.

'But it can't be,' I said aloud to myself. 'They're only skimpy little laces.' I gave them another tug, and then I found that I could hardly breathe. I knew what I had to do. I had to cut the laces. Pete's house is not a place where you can depend on finding a pair of scissors. I daresay I could have unearthed some if I'd turned the place upside down, but there wasn't time for that. I was beginning to feel faint. I stumbled down the stairs, thinking: I must get to the knives. I can cut the laces with a kitchen knife. That was the last thought I remember. I must have passed out then. When I woke up, I was lying on the floor of the hall with my head in Greg's lap. He was muttering softly and holding a wet cloth to my forehead.

'Oh, Bella!' he said when I opened my eyes. 'Oh, Bella, we all thought you were dead!'

I could hardly speak. I only said, 'Get my belt off, Greg, quickly. Please. Cut the laces.'

Greg didn't move. Pete ran to fetch the sharpest kitchen knife and at last the belt was off. I could breathe again. As I began to feel better, I saw that all seven of the band were gathered around me.

'You okay now?' Pete asked. I nodded.

'What happened to the cat?' I said. 'There was a white cat in the hall before . . . ' My voice faded.

'Haven't seen a cat,' said Steve. The cat must have slipped out with Em. Em. Did she know she was making the belt impossible to remove? Could she have wanted me to faint, or worse? It seemed extremely unlikely to me, and yet every time I've thought about it since, the whole thing seems to have been intentional, as though she meant to do me harm. I know all the objections to such thoughts. Why should a perfect stranger want to hurt me? I have gone over and over it in my mind since yesterday and the answer I keep returning to is this: maybe Em is not a stranger but someone known to me. She did, after all, remind me of Marjorie. Could it have been Marjorie herself, in some kind of disguise, or is that paranoia? How, I asked myself for the hundredth time, could Marjorie have found out where I really was, and then all of a sudden I had the answer. Armand, the hairdresser we both went to . . . he could easily have told her. I cursed myself for being too talkative, and for not swearing him to secrecy. I could imagine the scene perfectly. Marjorie saying, 'Oh, I hardly see Bella these days, now she's so grown-up,' and Armand, right on cue, answering: 'Oh, but she was 'ere last week, and full of the beans, with Pete and the crazy loony house in World's End, I think she say . . .' and Marjorie would mutter: 'You're only young once,' or something similar, and then she'd walk the streets of World's End and once she'd come across Aladdin's Cave she'd know (because she knows me very well) that I would go in there all the time . . . the rest is easy. After all, Jeannie hadn't said how long Em had been one of her suppliers.

'Greg,' I said. 'Greg, listen. I think my stepmother is trying to kill me.'

Greg looked up from his guitar. 'I like that,' he said, smiling. 'That's a good one, even for you. Fancy a cup of coffee, my poor little tragedy queen?'

'You're hopeless,' I said. 'You have no imagination. Yes, I'll have a coffee. While you're making it, I shall fester and lurk. So be quick.'

I could hear Greg chuckling as he took the steps down to the kitchen in great flying leaps.

I didn't ask what he'd done with the pink suede belt, but I never saw it again.

This is a story my father used to tell me over and over again when I was a little girl. It's about my mother. When she was pregnant with me, he took her to see *Gone With the Wind* at the cinema. My mother loved going to the pictures better than anything. They would sit and hold hands and know that when the ruched silky curtain went up, when the darkness fell, the white screen would glow with light and they would be transported into an enchanted land where women were always lovely and perfectly dressed, and where one could tell the difference between a hero and a villain immediately, just by looking at them. When *Gone With the Wind* appeared, it was a sensation. This film was longer, more colourful, bigger in every way than any other picture anyone had seen. The American Civil War raged, the city of Atlanta burned, Tara was destroyed, people loved and lost and loved again, and towering over everything were the hero and heroine: Rhett Butler and Scarlett O'Hara.

It was wintertime when my parents saw the film, and the ground was covered in snow when they came out. They walked round to the car park at the back of the cinema. At one point, my mother slipped a little and put out her hand to prevent herself from falling. She wasn't badly hurt, but the tips of her fingers were slightly grazed. When they reached the car, my father tied his white handkerchief round my mother's hand.

'Just like those poor wounded soldiers in the film,' she said.

They drove home through the black night.

'Look at that snow!' my mother said. 'How white it is! Vivien Leigh looks wintery, doesn't she . . .? all that lovely white skin and hair like the night.' She laughed. 'I'd like our baby to look like that,' she said, turning to my father. 'Hair like the night, and skin like the snow, and lips as red as the blood on this hankie.'

When I was a little girl and my father was telling me this story, he'd always take me over to the mirror and show me my own face. The mirror always said the same thing, and I'd repeat the words silently in my head as I looked at my image in the glass: 'Hair like the night, skin like the snow and lips as red as blood.'

I resemble, of course, not Vivien Leigh at all, but my mother. It was only to be expected. As my father used to say to me until Marjorie came along:

'Your mother was more beautiful than any actress. And you are just like her.'

That was before his second marriage, before Marjorie.

Some people say they can remember being in their mother's womb, but I take that kind of statement with a couple of hefty pinches of salt. I think I can remember the three years between when I was two and when I was five, but it may just be that my father has told me so often about everything we did that it's become vivid to me in retrospect. Still, if anyone ever asked me to describe what life was like before my father's second marriage, I'd have all the answers.

We lived in a big, comfortable, shabby sort of house with a big, comfortable, shabby sort of garden around it. My father is a doctor. The only respectable rooms in the house were his surgery (to the left of the front door) and his little waiting room (to the right) with its hunting prints on the wall and its shiny copies of *Punch* and the *Illustrated London News* on a small table by the window. We didn't have a proper receptionist then. Mrs McBride, who kept house for us and cooked for us, used to stick her head round the door and call the patients into the surgery one by one.

My father must have been busy. Doctors are always busy. And yet, I remember flying kites on Wimbledon Common. He would put me on his shoulders and run and run and I'd cling on to his hair, and the wind would lift the bright orange diamond of our kite up and up until I was sure it would touch a cloud, and all the time he'd never stop running and the green earth would tilt and fall away, far, far below me, and every minute I felt as though we were going to run right off the edge of the turning world. I remember that. I also remember being pushed on the baby swing in the park, and squelching along to the shops in my wellington boots, hoping my father was going to buy some liquorice all-sorts for us to share on the way home. I even remember the bedtime songs. Every night, he would sing three songs: 'Bye bye blackbird', 'When the red red robin comes bob-bob-bobbin' along' and 'Golden Slumbers'. Then he would say:

'Would you like two more?' and I would nod and he would do his encores, always the same songs in the same order: 'Over the Rainbow' and 'If you were the only girl in the world'. By the time I was three I could sing all of them perfectly and would give concerts in the waiting room almost daily. The patients loved me. So did Mrs McBride. So, more than any of them, did my father.

Before his second marriage, there was always music playing in our house. My father loved jazz and taught me how to find my way through the woefully wailing saxophones, the silver trumpets and the syncopated rhythms of the piano. Then I listened to the voices. I heard the blues: Bessie Smith, Leadbelly, and most loved of all, Billie Holiday, Lady Day, with a gardenia in her hair and songs that yearned and swooped and lodged themselves in the dark corners of my heart. I pretended to be her. I tucked a dead chrysanthemum (the nearest thing I could find to a gardenia) behind my ear and sang along to all her records.

Alice and Megan can never understand why I'm so mad about music. Alice's mother plays the piano, but the way I listen to Radio Lux under the bedclothes mystifies them. They keep up with all the latest songs, because simply being a friend of mine is an education in pop music. I'm always singing and they're always listening, but their hearts aren't in it. They simply cannot see what I see in Elvis, for instance. Alice thinks he looks horrible, with 'thick, blubbery lips' as she puts it, and his music is 'too noisy'. Megan thinks he's a little ridiculous. She doesn't actually say so, but I can tell. She finds him funny. When she and Alice mention the name of one of his songs, I can hear the inverted commas in their voices as they say the words aloud.

I love Elvis because he came along to help me when I particularly wanted to annoy Marjorie. He was louder and more dangerous-looking than Buddy Holly. I stuck posters of him all over my bedroom at home and played his records at full blast on my portable gramophone. Marjorie winced and frowned every time she came into my bedroom and found me gyrating to the pounding rhythms of his guitar. Thank you, Elvis, I used to think, and cherished him for being everything Marjorie couldn't stand: wild and slightly greasy and the possessor of a Pelvis that upset her very much.

One night when I was four, my father went to a Fancy Dress dance at the Bridge Club and met Marjorie. He fell in love with her from the very first moment he saw her, shimmying away in a beaded 1920s-style gown that clung to every bit of her. I mustn't let my present feelings for Marjorie obscure the truth about her. She is very beautiful, even now, and in those days her loveliness was the kind that made people, men and women, stare after her in the street. She was – is – as tall as my father, and a sort of goldy-brown colour all over. Her hair is tawny and thick, and she has always worn it in a page-boy bob to just above her shoulders. Her clothes tend towards the golden, too. Shiny fabrics and velvety ones, softly draped and clingy, are what she likes: silk jersey and crêpe and evening dresses made of satin that slide over her body like licks of gloss paint.

My father thought she was wonderful. He brought her to the house and *I* thought she was wonderful. She used to stand me on the padded stool in front of my own mother's dressing-table mirror and pat my nose with fluffy puffs of sweet-smelling face powder. She used to hang chains around my neck and let me clop around the house in her high-heeled shoes. She let me open her handbag and take out her ruby-studded compact and her lipstick and pretend to use them.

She made gradual changes in the house. She changed the pictures in the waiting room. She tidied up – oh, not by herself, but she saw to it. Mrs McBride vanished and was replaced by Mrs Deering, a thin-faced, sour woman who for the most part kept herself to herself.

My father told me when I was five what was going to happen.

'There's going to be a lovely wedding party,' he said, 'and you shall be the only bridesmaid. Then after that, Marjorie will come and live here and she'll be your very own new mummy.'

'And we'll have such fun together, darling, won't we?' added Marjorie, crushing me against her fragrant bosom. 'The very first thing we must do is decide on the dresses . . . yours and mine.'

It was the happiest day of my life. The next few weeks

were most tremendously exciting. I trailed around every-where with Marjorie: to the dressmakers, the shoe shops, the jewellers, the florists, and everywhere we went, everyone would make a fuss of me and give me little presents and kiss me.

Very occasionally I take out the photograph album with the wedding pictures in it, looking to see if there's any sign at all there of Marjorie's dislike of me, or of my feelings towards her. My dress was very pale blue, I remember, and I had a little coronet of pale blue flowers on my head. The cake had four tiers. Marjorie wore a dress in oyster satin, very closely draped round every curve of her body, and there were quite a few of those. My father's eyes are fixed on her in every single picture. I don't know who took the photographs, but it seems as if I was trying to attract his attention. I'm smiling very winsomely, straight at the camera. Everyone looks blissfully happy, just as though bad thoughts, unhappiness and jealousy were only to be found somewhere else. Not here. Never here.

I don't think I realized, then, that Marjorie would be with us the whole time. I think I thought that she would go back to her own house to sleep. I said so to my father one day and he laughed.

'But she's my wife now, Bella darling. I love her.'

'You said you loved me.' (I know I must have been pouting as I said this. I was tearing up my toast at the time.)

'I *do* love you, Bella. I love you best in the world, you know that. *Do* you know that?'

'Yes,' I said, 'but what about Mummy?'

My father sighed. 'I did love Mummy, but she would want Marjorie to look after us both now that she's not here any more.'

My father was right. Marjorie did look after us. The house was redecorated. The garden was landscaped. A receptionist was installed in the waiting room behind a desk. Later on, my father's surgery was moved to another part of London altogether because, as Marjorie put it:

'Seeing patients in one's own house is too, too A.J. Cronin for words.'

I didn't know it then, but soon discovered that A.J. Cronin wrote books about Scottish doctors whose one desire was to help the poor.

Marjorie arranged flowers in large and (I thought) rather ugly vases all over the house. Women with jewellery that rattled came to play bridge and take tea. We hardly ever went for walks or flew kites. My father was too successful, and in any case, by then I was too old to be put up on his shoulders, and too old to be sung to at night. There were no more bed-time songs.

People don't realize, I think, quite how much little children notice. I knew, right from the start, that my father enjoyed the way Marjorie snuggled against him when they kissed. He liked her to lean round him as he sat at breakfast, and kiss him on the mouth and rub her blouse against his shoulder. I could see that he liked touching her, and it didn't surprise me at all. I liked touching her too. Her skin was smooth and silky and she smelled lovely. I told Megan and Alice once that I'd wanted to learn French ever since I heard the beautiful names of Marjorie's perfumes said aloud: 'Je Reviens' and 'Arpège' and 'Jolie Madame' and my favourite, 'Vent Vert' which, she said, meant Green Wind.

She had the most wonderful underwear I'd ever seen. It was, all of it, lacy and delicate and slippery, and it lay quietly in her drawers until the moment came for dressing, when it would unfold into foaming waves of peach or white or black against Marjorie's skin.

'When I'm a big lady,' I used to say, 'I'm going to have things exactly like that.' But years later, when we went to Daniel Neal's, in order to kit me out ready for Egerton Hall, I nearly wept with rage, right there in the shop. All those horrid thick cotton knickers and beige socks and hideously scratchy liberty bodices filled me with despair. I looked at Marjorie as if to say: help me. You know I loathe this. Help me not to have to go to a place that makes you wear knickers like these. Marjorie, though, had started to hate me long before I went away to school and the only expression to cross her face was a smile of undisguised triumph.

Maybe I'm being melodramatic again, and half of it is in my own mind, but this I do know. Marjorie's attitude towards me changed when I was seven. I can pinpoint the very day: it was the day of my first visit to Monsieur Armand's hair-dressing salon, Chez Armand. Up until then, Marjorie loved me in the way that someone loves a pretty doll. She liked dressing me up in lovely clothes. She even enjoyed draping me in her own jewels and scarves and spraying me with perfume from the cut-glass bottles lining the dressing-table. When it came to matters of style or make-up, she was a talented teacher. There are things she said then which had the force of moral rules for her: you must never wear a white blouse over black underwear, you must never wear high-heeled shoes with trousers, you must never wear a cardigan over a cotton dress, and you must never be seen in your dressing-gown after ten in the morning unless you were ill, and you must always, always assume, every single time you left the house (even if you were just popping down the road to post a letter) that on this occasion you would meet someone of the utmost importance, like the Man of Your Dreams or a Crowned Head of Europe. You also had to take it for granted that every time you left the house you were going to be the victim of an accident and doctors saving your life would furrow their brows in deep distress if your vest was less than pristine and ditto, naturally, your knickers.

When I was seven, Marjorie decided that I looked wild.

'Look, darling,' she said to my father one night. 'Bella's turning into a little ragamuffin. You don't want to be a little ragamuffin, Bella dear, do you?'

'No,' I answered, a bit doubtfully. Secretly I thought a ragamuffin sounded rather nice, like a tastier version of a muffin.

'Tomorrow,' Marjorie continued, 'I shall take you to meet Monsieur Armand, my divine hairdresser, and we'll ask his advice. Monsieur Armand always knows exactly what to do. And won't you be glad to be rid of all that messy hair? To say nothing of the time we shall save, not having to plait it every morning before school.'

I thought: she never does plait it, anyway. It's always Mrs Deering who does it.

Stepping into Chez Armand was like walking into the heart of a rose. The carpets were pink and soft, the chairs were covered in pink velvet. I was very impressed when a pretty lady put some cushions on a chair and lifted me on to them. She then covered me with a pink sheet, so that only my head was showing. I giggled and said to Marjorie:

'My head looks like a black cherry on top of a pink blancmange.'

Marjorie wasn't listening. She was smiling and waving at someone she knew on the other side of the salon. I didn't care. I was looking at the enormous mirror in front of me. It had the most wonderful golden frame carved with roses, long, trailing ribbons, leaves, little vases, a musical instrument I'd never seen before, and at the very top, a couple of chubby naked babies who made me smile. I realized, because of their wings, that they were meant to be little angels, but they still struck me as fat and funny, flying about at the top of the mirror with not even nappies to cover their bottoms.

After a while, Monsieur Armand arrived for The Consultation.

'Mais *elle est tellement mignonne*!' he exclaimed. I didn't know at the time what this meant, but I gathered he liked me, because he kept blowing kisses at my reflection in the mirror.

'Well, yes,' Marjorie said, a little shaken by all this ecstasy, 'but she does look rather untidy, don't you think? What should we do?'

'Perhaps,' Monsieur Armand considered carefully, 'a little fringe *comme ça*, and just below the ears like that?'

'That sounds very nice,' said Marjorie and pulled up a velvet chair so that she could follow every snip. My black hair fell on to the pink sheet like feathers. I didn't like it at first: the horrible, softly crunching sound the scissors made as they closed on my hair. But after a while, and soothed by Monsieur Armand's gentle murmurings and his strong hands turning my head first this way then that, I began to relax and enjoy myself.

'When I'm a grown-up lady,' I told Monsieur Armand, 'I shall come in here every single week to have my hair done just like Marjorie.'

Marjorie leaned forward so that her head was reflected next to mine in the mirror.

'What do you think, Armand, do I need a trim? Or perhaps a set?'

'Reassure yourself, Madame,' Monsieur Armand smiled at her. 'You are looking . . . how do you say? A picture. Perhaps a set in a day or so?'

'I'll make an appointment on the way out.'

'*Voilà!*' He turned to Marjorie with a flourish, to show her the result of his labours on me. 'Do you not think this is *merveilleux*?'

'Oh, that's very nice,' said Marjorie. 'Thank you so much, Armand.'

'Thank you,' I said. 'I think it's lovely.'

'You are going to become . . . how do you say? . . . the competition for Madame Lavanne, *n'est-çe pas*?'

Marjorie was almost silent on the way home. My father was very pleased with my new hair-style.

'You look simply lovely, Bellissima!' he said and kissed me. 'More like your mother than ever. It quite takes me back!' Maybe his words were less than diplomatic. Marjorie became even quieter.

'Ooh, the little pet!' said Mrs Deering when she saw me. 'Doesn't she look a picture?' Mrs Deering was a glum woman usually and this uncharacteristic enthusiasm reduced Marjorie to total silence.

At the time, I didn't really notice that Marjorie was in a sulk. I was so excited that I could hardly tear myself away from the mirror. I was sitting at Marjorie's dressing-table and gloating, when she came into the room and saw me, and started shaking.

'I don't know whose dressing-table you think this is, young lady,' she said in a wobbly voice, 'but I'd rather you didn't use it from now on, d'you hear?'

I jumped down from the stool and started to make my way to the door. I'd never seen Marjorie like this. She went on:

'It's mine. It's *my* dressing-table, and you're to keep away from it, do you understand?'

'Yes, Marjorie,' I whispered, nearly at the door. She was coming towards me now. She said:

'Haven't you got a mirror in your bedroom?'

'Yes,' I whispered.

'Then bloody well use it in future!' She pushed me a little roughly out of the door and banged it behind me. I felt icy all over. I wanted to run and tell my father, but I knew that I mustn't do that: it'd only make things worse. I wanted to open the door and run to Marjorie and ask her what had happened, and why she wasn't being nice to me any more and what had I done to stop her liking me, and wasn't she going to be my mother any longer? At the same time, I wanted to hit her and hurt her and break every single bottle on her dressing-table into tiny pieces and cover her carpet with broken glass. I did none of those things. I just stood there, paralysed, and then I heard a strange noise coming from inside the door. It sounded just like . . . but it couldn't be, because grown-ups never cried, did they? I looked through the keyhole and saw Marjorie staring into the mirror and howling like a child, tears running down her face and into her neck and she wasn't even bothering to wipe them away. I ran to my own room and closed the door and didn't come out again until supper-time.

Marjorie looked fairly normal during the meal, and spoke fairly normally too, but we knew, both of us, that something between us had changed that day.

What I still think of as The Snowflake Campaign started soon after our visit to Monsieur Armand's salon.

Snowflake was my cat. By the time Marjorie came to live in the house, she was already a grown-up, sedate sort of cat, much given to flopping about on carpets and curling up on the quilt on my bed. She padded about the house, looking wistfully at Mrs Deering as she cooked, or sat for hours on the windowsill in my bedroom, remembering her younger days, when she used to chase squirrels up into the trees with great abandon. She was white and fluffy, with eyes the colour of boiled gooseberries. I loved her. My father had given her to me for my second birthday, and he loved her too. She slept on my bed, usually quite placidly by my toes, but in winter I'd often wake up and find she was occupying half the pillow.

Marjorie never seemed to mind Snowflake, although I don't think she was ever mad about her. She never seemed to stroke her, Mrs Deering and I fed her, and really, I would have said that Marjorie hardly knew Snowflake was in the house. Then, one morning, The Campaign began. Marjorie arrived at the breakfast-table dabbing her eyes with a lace-edged hankie.

'I cannot seem,' she said to my father, 'to stop my eyes watering. Do you think I could be allergic to something?' My father munched toast rapidly and answered, not even looking at Marjorie properly:

'I expect it's all that muck you put on your eyes, dear. Mascara and what-have-you. Terrifically delicate things, eyes.' Marjorie stabbed at the butter and took the severed lump on to her plate. Her hand, I could see, was trembling but her voice was as sweet and clear as the Golden Shred marmalade she was busy applying to her toast.

'I hardly think so, Robert. I have, after all, been wearing this make-up with no ill-effects for years and years.'

'Then perhaps,' said my father, 'it's a slight cold coming on. Or even hay fever. There's a tremendous amount of hay fever about this year.'

'If you want my opinion,' said Marjorie, 'I think it's the cat.'

She always called Snowflake 'the cat'. I thought: how would she like it if Snowflake, or anyone else, for that matter, called her 'the woman'? My father pushed his chair away from the table.

'We'll talk about it tonight, darling. I have to rush now, truly. Though I can't imagine who would want to be allergic to poor old Snowflake, what?' He laughed.

'People do not choose, Robert, what they are allergic to. The reaction simply happens, whether you want it to or not. As a doctor, you should know that.'

'I do, my blossom, I do!' My father blew kisses in the general direction of both of us as he left the room. When he'd gone, Marjorie turned to me.

'Why, Bella dear, are you looking at me like that?' she said.

'I'm not, Marjorie,' I said quickly. 'Honestly, I'm not.' I bent my head and looked very closely at my plate. But I *was* looking. I had seen two things. Firstly, that Marjorie's eyes were now completely non-inflamed, and secondly, that Snowflake had come silently into the room and was now asleep behind the fruit bowl on the sideboard, within about two feet of where Marjorie was sitting.

For the next couple of weeks, she sniffed and coughed and wiped her eyes and assured my father (who was meanwhile treating her for hay fever) that Snowflake was the cause of her increasing discomfort.

I never imagined my poor cat was in any danger. They waited, my father and Marjorie, until I was safely at school, and then they murdered her. Oh, I don't mean they cut her throat with a razor or anything like that. No. Of course not. They simply took her to the vet, and she was put to sleep.

That was how my father told me, when I came back from school at lunchtime.

'We had to put her to sleep, lovey,' he said. 'She was making poor Marjorie ill.'

'But couldn't she just have gone to live somewhere else? With another family?' I wailed.

'No, Bella, she would have been very unhappy. Cats grow attached to their houses, their territory, you know. It's better this way.'

'Then why didn't you say you were going to do it? I never even kissed her goodbye! You're cruel and horrible and I hate you both.'

'Bella darling, don't say that! We didn't tell you because we didn't want to make you unhappy.'

'But you have!' I shrieked. 'You *have* made me. Very, very unhappy. I'm not going to stop crying. Not ever, so there.'

I did stop crying. Of course I did. Everything calmed down after a while, as it always does. But I have not forgotten that day. If I'd believed, really believed that Marjorie was allergic to cats, then maybe I would have been more sympathetic, but I think, even after all these years, that she made it up. She did it to hurt me. I don't think allergies had anything to do with it. After all, she has always worn her leopard-skin coat with no ill-effects. Poor leopards, killed to make coats for people like Marjorie! And poor Snowflake, now only a smudgy white blur in a few tiny photographs in my album.

Marjorie became subtle after a while and so did I. She realized quickly that my father loved the idea of the two of us being the best of friends, so that was what she pretended to be. Everyone admired her for it. Everyone was taken in by it, except me. Oh, she let me go back to sitting in front of her mirror and trying on her clothes and make-up, and she made a point of helping me to choose my clothes, and I, for my part, tried hard to annoy her without the whole thing becoming too obvious and thus calling the attention of my father to the sad fact that we were not, as he would put it, 'getting on'.

Visits to the hairdresser continued, of course, and each time we went, Marjorie would ask Monsieur Armand, sometimes in a roundabout way and sometimes straight out, which one of us was the more beautiful. For a long time, Monsieur Armand twisted and turned his replies into complicated knots of words that always worked out as the message Marjorie wanted to hear: there's nothing to choose between you. Then, one day when I was ten, she caught him off guard.

'Tell me truly, Armand,' she said after a particularly successful session with the scissors and rollers, 'how does the competition look now?' I was reading the *Tatler* in the velvet chair next to Marjorie's. Monsieur Armand looked across at me and then back at Marjorie's reflection in the mirror.

'You will 'ave,' he said with a shrug, 'to . . . as you say, I think . . . look to the laurels.'

Marjorie's anguished stare nearly shattered the glass. We left the salon quickly. I knew better than to ask Marjorie herself what 'look to the laurels' meant. Later that evening, I asked Mrs Deering. She said:

'Well, it's like a championship, you know. You got the laurels as a prize, see, and if someone coming up was going to be even better, you had to jolly well look out, make sure this other person didn't win your laurels off you. Do you understand?'

I understood very well indeed. It meant that Monsieur Armand thought I was going to be prettier than Marjorie. And Marjorie, although she couldn't really hurt me, was from that moment deeply against me. She would never show it, but I knew. And although Megan and Alice don't believe me, I'm of the firm opinion that she tried to lose me at the Harrods sale.

'No one,' Megan said, 'takes a child to Harrods and deliberately loses her. It's ridiculous.'

I suppose she may be right, but I still remember how terrified I was.

We had gone up to Knightsbridge on the top of a number 73 bus. I loved it up there, seeing the whole of London spread out below me, and I loved Harrods. It smelled just like Marjorie's bedroom, only more so. It was always crowded, and most of the people were much taller than me, so that I felt that I was walking through a forest where the trees were moving about all around me. There were ladies in fur coats and gentlemen in suits all coming and going at great speed up and down the aisles. I must have been a nuisance to Marjorie. I must have slowed her down. I wanted to look at every single thing.

'May I stay here while you do the shopping, Marjorie?' I asked, when we reached Perfumery, my favourite department. Marjorie looked all around her, worried, as though dangerous kidnappers were hiding behind every marble column.

'I'm not a baby,' I said. 'I'm ten. I won't get lost. I'll stay here all the time.'

'Well, please see that you do, Bella. I shan't be long. I have to go to the Food Hall and the lingerie department, that's all, and then I'll come back and fetch you. I shan't be more than half an hour or so.'

'Oh, thank you,' I said, and she strode off to the Food Hall without a backward glance. After she had gone, I wondered how I was going to know when the half-hour was up. Then I had a brilliant idea. I asked the pretty lady behind the Revlon counter what the time was.

'It's eleven o'clock,' she said, and smiled.

I pottered about happily among the lipsticks and creams for what seemed like ages. I asked the pretty lady the time again, and she said:

'It's quarter to twelve.'

Marjorie was late. I wasn't really worried. Marjorie was often late. I found a little stool and sat down to wait. At half-past twelve I began to worry and at one o'clock I started to cry. My pretty friend came out from behind her counter to ask me what the matter was.

'It's Marjorie,' I sobbed. 'She's left me here. She's forgotten all about me.'

'Who's Marjorie?'

'My stepmother,' I said.

'She'll be back soon. You dry your eyes, love.'

'But she said half an hour and it's two hours. I want to go home.' I started howling in a way that simply wasn't done at Harrods. Someone called the Floor Manager came and took me into an office and I phoned my father in his surgery. I had never done such a thing before.

'I'm coming for you at once, Bella,' he said on the telephone. 'Stop crying and wait for me.'

I stopped crying and turned my attention to the milk and biscuits the Floor Manager had brought me.

My father hugged me at first, but later, in the car going home, he became angry when I told him the truth. I'd calmed down completely by then.

'However did you manage to get yourself lost?' he asked.

'I wasn't lost,' I said. 'I was exactly where I said I'd be. Marjorie forgot about me, that's all. I expect she wanted to lose me altogether.'

I think my father would have smacked me then, if he hadn't been driving the car. As it was, he flashed a furious glance in my direction and said, in the coldest voice I'd ever heard him use to me:

'Don't you *dare* say such a wicked thing, Bella! Apologize at once. I'm deeply, deeply ashamed of you. How could you even think such a thing?'

'I'm sorry,' I muttered. 'I shouldn't have said that.' Well, I certainly shouldn't have said it, but I wasn't in the least sorry. I knew I was right. We arrived home to find Marjorie in floods of tears, babbling on about how I'd wandered off and how she couldn't find me, and didn't know what to do, and how she'd run home in a panic and oh, poor love, how dreadful it must have been, and all the time she was weeping and clasping me to her bosom and saying how love-ly it was that everything had ended happily and on and on and on. But she didn't fool me, not for a moment. I could see right through to the coldness at the heart of her, and I knew, I could feel in the way she stroked my hair that some huge, hidden, iceberg-like part of her was deeply sorry that I had ever been 'found', as she put it, and brought home.

'And that's why,' I used to say to Megan and Alice, 'I was sent to Egerton Hall, don't you see? So that she could be rid of me. It was supposed to be a kind of exile. I could easily have gone to school round the corner from our house, but Marjorie wanted me far away.'

'But you like it here, don't you?' Alice said. 'It's not a bad kind of exile, is it?'

'Not bad at all, but the point is, Marjorie wouldn't care either way. I'm not where she is, that's the main thing. She likes to think of this place as set in the middle of a forest. That's what it said in the prospectus, anyway. She likes to pretend that I'm really hidden away. She was a bit disappointed when she saw what the real forest looked like!'

We all laughed then. Our forest, out beyond the school boundary (which we call The Rim of the Known World), *is* a bit of a joke. It's a scrubby sort of place with too few trees to score more than about four out of ten in a Sinister Forest Test. Still, it was the best Marjorie could do, and she approached my departure for Egerton Hall with more enthusiasm and pleasure than I'd seen her display in years.

I've been in bed thirty-six hours, which was about twenty-four hours longer than necessary, but I'm fully recovered now. Pete decided that we should have a special meal as a celebration of the fact that I was now well enough to cook it.

'I did all the shopping,' said Steve. 'I expect to be let off all the cooking and washing up.'

'Expect away,' I said. 'They'll rope you in.' Steve was a plump, dour sort of person, who didn't say much unless he was pointing out some grievance.

'Look at me,' I said. 'I'm not grumbling and I've got to fling together a delicious forgetti Bolognese, as Harry calls it, for eight people.'

'But you're a girl,' said Dave.

'And a trainee knife-thrower to boot,' I said, 'so I advise you not to make remarks like that in this kitchen when I'm around.'

'You are not,' said Pete to Dave, 'to fluster the cook. Gallons of gallant suffragette blood run in her veins, and if you're not good and polite she will dash off and chain herself to the nearest railing and then you can forget about forgetti, Bolognese or no Bolognese.'

I set about chopping onions and peppers and mushrooms

and soon the kitchen was full of fragrant steam rising from my saucepan.

Phil, a lanky man with a rather thin, high voice and toffee-coloured hair in a sort of mop-shape, had been sent down the road to the off-licence to get some bottles of wine. This was because the meal was a celebration. On non-celebration nights, they all drank beer and I generally had to make do with milk or water.

I doled out the spaghetti to everyone. 'Being mother' was what Dave called it.

'Not mother,' I grinned at him. 'Table Prefect. And if you don't behave yourselves, you can come and see me in my study after supper. I could give you Automatically Minus Two.'

'Ooh,' said Harry, 'that sounds lovely! Is it the name for a new sexual perversion?'

'No, stupid. You have Minus House Points and Plus House Points and at the end of term the House with the most points wins a cup.'

Kenny said, 'How too, too Malory Towers, darling!' and stretched his arms languidly above his head, and everyone laughed and said: 'Jolly hockey sticks!' and 'St Trinian's!' and I ignored them and continued to dole out spaghetti.

'Shut up and eat your supper,' I said.

'Only if you swear to tell us what you all got up to after Lights Out, treasure,' said Kenny. I stuck my tongue out at him, and tossed a piece of bread at his head, but it missed and hit Dave instead. We all started giggling then, and Phil and Steve began to suck up individual strands of spaghetti.

'You're nothing but a bunch of silly kids,' I said, 'and you're the ones who are going to have to clean up this mess. Greg and I have things to discuss.'

Wolf whistles, shouts of 'Hello, hello, what's this then?'

and hoots of one kind and another greeted this remark. Greg turned redder than the Bolognese sauce and said:

'I've written a couple of songs for Bella to sing. We want to rehearse them, that's all.'

'Well, ducky,' said Kenny, 'I've heard plenty of euphemisms in my time, but rehearsing's a good one, I have to admit.'

'When I get my hands on you, Kenny,' I smiled, 'you'll have to think of a euphemism for strangling.'

Kenny laughed. 'Can't think of anything in the world more titillating than being manhandled by a public school-girl. I can hardly wait, darling. Do come over here and start.' I ignored him and finished my spaghetti. Greg smiled at me gratefully. I had succeeded in diverting everyone's attention from him, so he could listen to the banter quite happily.

There always was a lot of chatting and laughter at the table, but it struck me as I watched them that these seven supposedly grown-up men, living in suitably beatnik disorder, actually had as many rules and regulations governing their meals as we had at Egerton Hall, even if the table manners that went with them left something to be desired. They did a great deal of slouching about, loud laughing, chucking around of bits of bread, and passing salt and pepper pots across your face when your spoon was an inch away from your mouth. Still, every one of the band had his appointed seat at the table, and I had to learn which mug was whose very quickly because no one would dream of taking even one sip from somebody else's.

Phil, Dave and Harry did the washing-up. On the table, the candle we'd stuck into the Chianti bottle to be extra festive had burned down to its last inch, and the green glass was encrusted with opaque white blobs and bobbles and streaks of hardened wax.

Monday morning and the house is empty and everything is slightly different after the weekend. Megan came to stay for a couple of days, and now she's gone there's a chance to think. While she was here, we were too busy talking. I only told her briefly about the pink suede belt – I'd almost begun to think I'd imagined it, anyway.

'We'll take turns,' I said. 'You can have the chaise-longue on alternate nights.'

'It's okay,' said Megan. 'My sleeping-bag's probably more comfortable, especially if I lie it on top of a folded blanket or something.'

'I know,' I said. 'That's why I want to alternate. In a previous incarnation, this chaise-longue was used as a kind of rack by the Spanish Inquisition.' We started to giggle. I said:

'It'll be just like the Tower Room, but with fags.'

'Oh, no, Bella. Not fags. You know I hate the smell.'

'The whole house reeks of smoke, though. What will you do?'

'Suffer, I suppose. But I'm going to make you hang out of the window in here. I don't see why I should have smoke puffed right in my face.'

I wasn't really listening to her. I said:

'It won't really be like the Tower Room. Alice isn't here.'

'No,' said Megan, and then, 'Do you think about her a lot?'

'All the time. You?'

'Yes,' said Megan. 'I feel sick when I think about it. I feel cold and terrified.'

'I don't. I feel hot and angry. I feel I'd like to hit someone very hard. Him, preferably.'

I meant Angus. I couldn't even remember exactly what he looked like, except that he was dark and had eyebrows that met above his nose. Megan shook her head as if to clear it of terrible thoughts, and sat down on a reasonably clean bit of floor. She said:

'I like this house. Dorothy would have fifty fits if she could see me.'

I laughed aloud. Dorothy was Megan's guardian, a frosty, stuffy sort of person. I said:

'What about Marjorie? She'd have a hundred fits if she could see me. It's super fun that you could come. And extra super that it's this weekend. You can come to The Dance.'

'What dance? You never said anything about a dance. I haven't brought a dress.'

'You don't need a dress. You're coming with us. You can be like one of the band. Your blue skirt'll be fine, and that silky blouse. We can go down to Jeannie's and pick you up a piece of glittery jewellery, if you like.'

'I don't like. Honestly, Bella, you might have told me! I don't even know if I want to go to this dance. Where is it?'

'It's being given in this amazingly posh enormous house in Cheyne Gardens. A twenty-first birthday party for the Hon. Roderick Maxton. Everyone who is anyone will be there: the Jeunesse Dorée, the Bright Young Things, the Crème de la Crème . . .'

'You're trying to camouflage the fact,' said Megan, 'that this is actually some kind of debutantes' do, and the place will be crawling with chinless wonders, ninety per cent of whom will be called Nigel.'

I laughed.

'You're quite right,' I said. 'Thank goodness we're going with the band.'

Megan said, 'But what I don't understand is how the band, who all look so disreputable, get themselves invited to play at such a party.'

'Ah, well, that's Greg's doing. He and Miss Rilly Maxton used to have what Pete calls "a Thing". She used to be his girl-friend, and she's the Hon. Roderick's sister, so, of course . . .'

'Whatever kind of name is Rilly?' Megan wanted to know.

'Short for Amaryllis, wouldn't you just know it? She's actually quite pretty, but definitely the sort of person who looks as though she's just on the point of turning into a pig, like the baby in *Alice in Wonderland*. She's pink and healthy-looking and her nose turns up. I think I shall put it slightly out of joint when she realizes how Greg feels about me. According to Harry, who is an expert on these matters, Rilly still thinks Greg is (and I quote him) "hers".'

'Oh, well, if there are to be dramatic jealous scenes,' said Megan, 'then I'm quite looking forward to the occasion. By then I will have got used to the band myself. I was quite overwhelmed by them this morning. I felt like a nice, juicy bone in the midst of a bunch of over-eager puppies.'

It was true. They had all (apart from Greg, who stood alone outside the group, smiling) patted Megan and grinned at her, and pressed cups of coffee, cigarettes and biscuits at her, and pulled out chairs for her and jostled to be near her. In the end, I had to shoo them all away, or I would never have had a chance to talk to Megan myself.

'They were just excited, that's all,' I explained. 'They'll have calmed down by tonight. And when they're playing, when we're on – well, they'll take no notice of you whatso-ever. You could be doing the dance of the seven veils and they wouldn't even glance in your direction. They get swallowed up by the music.'

'Even Greg?' Megan asked and winked at me.

'Greg especially,' I said. 'Although I'm going to sing two of his songs for the very first time tonight, so he might just look up to see if they're okay.'

*

The Maxton house – they would probably have preferred it to be called the Maxton Residence – was huge. There was a flight of steps leading up to the front door, with fat white columns holding up the porch. We arrived before the guests, and Lady Maxton was all of a twitter.

'Vernon,' she trilled to a butlerish sort of person, 'these are the young people for the cellar.' She turned her hostess smile on us.

'Darlings, I do admire your costumes. Too, too Bohemian for words. Vernon will show you your "spot", as darling Roddy calls it. You'll never believe how the cellar's been transformed. Magic on the part of Belinda Sowersby – do you know her?'

We all trooped down to the cellar behind Vernon. I said to Megan:

'Costumes, indeed! What a cheek! These are the same clothes most of them have been in all day. I know for a fact that Kenny hasn't changed his shirt since Thursday. Bohemian, I ask you!'

The cellar had been made to look as much like a sleazy nightclub as Belinda Sowersby, whoever she was, could manage. There was a space for dancing, tables with red and white checked cloths on them, red light bulbs everywhere and candles stuck in bottles all over the place.

'Are we allowed to wander about, then?' I asked.

'I don't see why not,' Pete said. 'But be back here by twelve ready for work.'

'We'll stick out like sore thumbs,' said Megan as we came up from the cellar into the house.

'I don't care,' I said. 'I'm only looking.'

Rilly Maxton was in peacock blue satin, and Jennifer's Diary would undoubtedly refer to her in the next issue of *Tatler* as 'resplendent'. She did her best to corner Greg, but he slunk off and hid in the cellar and pretended to make last-minute adjustments to the microphone.

The house was full of dresses. Skirts in fondant colours, in soft, rustly materials, wispy chiffons and lustrous satins, stiff crinolines in glittery taffeta, moved in and out of doorways and round and round the dance floors, and every exotic flower of a skirt was tied, it seemed, to a black-and-white stake: a partner in evening dress. We made our way to where an enormously long table was spread with all the things which, as Megan put it, 'were our best fantasies at school'. We walked the length of this table, plucking vol-au-vents and legs of chicken and smoked salmon sandwiches from the plates as we passed. A sedate sort of orchestra (three elderly men in penguin suits and a white-haired lady in beaded aquamarine at the pianoforte) were squelching out Victor Sylvester imitations in the ballroom, which was about the size of a small cathedral, though more elaborately decorated.

Soon it was what Megan called 'Cinderella time' and we went down to the cellar again. It was packed. Couples were crowding the dance floor, all the girls in their pretty flowers of dresses by this time twined round their black-and-white men, clinging to them, making their arms into soft tendrils to bind round necks and waists. Music poured into the spaces around them, golden and sweet like treacle. Inhibitions had melted in the candle flames. Everywhere, couples were kissing, oblivious of the rest of the world.

I started out by singing some smoochy standards. Then, towards the end of my set, I sang one of the songs Greg had written for me:

> Pack your bags
> and all your money
> don't forget your jewels,

honey.
We're going to ride
that dazzle train
right into love
and back again.
Tell the guard
just where you're goin'
hear that lovesick
whistle blowin'.
Grab your sweetie,
hang on tight,
love train's goin' to
run all night.

The upbeat rhythm, the change of pace after all the smoochiness, made everyone pay attention. Even the most drowned of the kissers came up for air and looked at me. No one danced as I sang it, but on the reprise, someone started clapping to the beat, and everyone else joined in. When I finished the applause was deafening. I looked at Greg. I'd felt him smiling at my back all the time I'd been singing, but now his eyes were glittering most suspiciously.

'He was,' Megan told me much later. 'He was nearly crying as you sang.'

Pete jumped up and raised his hand for silence.

'Thanks, folks! We're glad you liked that song, because it was written by Greg, there on the guitar. Let's hear it for Greg!' (Another burst of applause.) 'But we've lost that loving, melancholy mood, it seems, so to bring it back, here's Bella again with another song by Greg. Quite a different one, this is. Take it away, Bella!'

I sang 'Turn your face' then and the words filled the air like smoke:

Turn your face,
turn your eyes,
turn yourself
to me.
What do you see,
tell me,
what do you see?
I see white birds flying
high into the blue.
I see all my sweet dreams
never coming true.
I see all your loving
walking out the door,
I hear goodbye words
you never said before.
You've met another someone
but don't you realize
you've got pieces of the past
pieces of my fantasies
pieces of my love for you
forever in your eyes.

'Greg,' I said to him as I stepped away from the microphone, 'thank you for those songs.' I could see he wanted to say something, but couldn't find words. He seemed to be reaching out for air. I said:

'When it's time for your break, let's have a drink.' He nodded and turned back to his guitar.

Later on, Greg and I had a glass of wine each, sitting at one of the tables. Suddenly, I felt a surge of tenderness and affection for him sweep over me. I put my hand over his.

'Greg, the songs are beautiful. Everyone really loved them.

I loved singing them.' Greg smiled and said nothing. Now, a tape recorder was playing 'Body and Soul'.

'Come,' I said, 'dance with me. It's ages since I danced with anyone.'

At first, he stood very stiffly, slightly away from me. I could feel the tension running all down his arm as it circled my waist. It seemed as though he'd stopped breathing. I said:

'Greg, this is like dancing with a suit of armour! What's the matter with you? I'm not made of china. I shan't break, you know.'

I deliberately put both my arms around his neck and moved my body close to his. I could feel tremors running through him at first, and then he stopped trembling and bent his head so that his mouth was buried in my hair. I closed my eyes.

Greg was very warm. I could feel his breath touching my forehead. I felt sleepy. I felt safe with his arms around me. I snuggled in closer to him. I felt so cosy there, so comfortable, so full of what I think must have been a kind of gratitude for his kindness, his love, his beautiful songs, that I lifted my face to his and kissed him very thoroughly on the mouth. It was as though I'd turned a tap, flicked a switch, opened the lid on a box of feelings that Greg had been keeping carefully hidden.

'Oh, Bella, Bella,' he said, almost sighing, and then he kissed me: my mouth, my hair, my neck where it met my shoulders: hundreds of kisses and words muttered under his breath so that I could hardly hear them. I caught 'so much'. I heard 'never' and 'always' and my name over and over again, and his arms were around me, unhesitatingly this time and tight, as if he never wanted to let me go.

*

'But do you love him?' Megan asked me the next afternoon. She had left her sleeping-bag. I was still on the chaise-longue.

'I like him. I like the way he makes me feel when he kisses me. He comforts me, just by being there. He makes me feel safe, cared for. I don't know. Would you call that love?'

Megan came over and sat on the end of the chaise-longue.

'I don't know either,' she said. 'But I think if you have to ask the question, then it may not be.'

'I don't care.' I grinned at her, feeling as though everything in the world were suddenly lit up. 'Even if it isn't love, it feels jolly nice. So there.'

'Then,' said Megan, 'you can tell for certain that it isn't love. Love means torment and anguish and suffering.' I jumped off the chaise-longue and pulled a face.

'That's a lot of flummery and flannel put about by the Romantic poets and I don't believe a word of it!' I ran up to the bathroom singing 'I'm in love with a wonderful guy' at the very top of my voice.

So now Greg and I will be considered A Couple. I don't know what I feel about this. I laughed it off with Megan, but in my heart of hearts, I know – I think I know – that what I feel for Greg isn't love. It isn't what the poets mean by love, it isn't what Elvis and Buddy Holly and Billie Holliday and all the songs mean by it. The truth of the matter is, I'm rather ignorant about Love and Sex and everything that goes with them, except in theory. Oh, I was considered (am still considered, probably) the expert on such matters at school. I have had a reputation since the Junior House for being daring, precocious, adventurous. I was the first person in the class to be kissed properly. I read all the juicy books first, and was quite clever about picking up the clues the writer let slip about the disposition of limbs, etc. etc. The truth of the matter is, Megan knows what there is to know and I only imagine it, and the irony is, I can't interrogate her about such matters, because I'm supposed to know already. In any case, Megan would find it hard, not so much to put what she felt into words, but to give a good, practical account of what actually happens: who does what and for how long and what does it feel like, when you get past all the grunting and heaving and melting and so forth that goes on in books? I shall have to find out for myself, I suppose, and the reason I know that what I feel for Greg isn't love is this: at the moment, anyway, I do not especially want him to be the one to teach me.

'But why ever not?' I imagine Megan saying. 'He's so handsome and sweet and he loves you so much.'

I don't know why not. Kissing him is very pleasant. He looks after me. He is devoted to me. Perhaps that's what's not right about it. I feel affectionate towards him, tender, concerned. I like stroking his hair. I've thought and thought about it, and decided that I am fond of Greg in much the same way as I'd be fond of a special pet. I do not feel swept off my feet, breathless, anxious, tremulous, in despair, and so I suppose I am not in love. If I had a proper mother, I'd ask her: how will I know when the real thing happens to me? I cannot tell what my real mother would have said, but Marjorie would trot out clichés from the latest magazine article. I can hear her now: 'Love will hit you when you least expect it.' She would probably start paraphrasing 'Some Enchanted Evening', which is a sort of National Anthem for believers in Love at First Sight. With a hey and a ho and a hey nonny no!

Later that week, over breakfast, Pete suddenly put down his paper and looked at all of us slouching round the table in various stages of undress. He said:

'Well, I can't think why when I look at you all, but I had a chat with Matt Quinton yesterday, and he's fixed up an engagement for us in Paris.'

Everyone who was eating stopped at once. Greg said:

'Paris? Are you serious? When?'

Pete laughed. 'Quite serious. There's a place in Montparnasse called Club Sortilège. Matt's dad is part-owner. They're offering us one spot per night. Money's not great, but it's Paris, so who cares, eh?'

'When is this?' I said.

'Next week. Can you make it, Bella? What about your folks? Will they mind?'

'I'll fix it,' I said, already composing in my head a suitable tissue of lies for the benefit of my father and Marjorie. 'Have you got an address I can give them? Parents always find that tremendously reassuring, for some reason.'

'That's the best bit,' said Pete. 'Free accommodation, and guess where?'

'Let me try,' said Kenny. 'What about wrapped in old copies of Le Figaro on top of the Metro gratings?'

'Close,' said Pete. 'It's an artist's studio.'

'What about the artist? Where will he be?'

'On holiday. Beside the sea.'

'Don't know what the world's coming to,' said Kenny. 'Time was when your artist would be slowly starving to death over a nice cosy glass of absinthe. Now they're traipsing off to the seaside like common or garden trippers. And does anyone speak French?'

'I do,' I said. 'I did it for my A-levels.'

'Thank goodness for that,' said Phil. 'The rest of us haven't got two sentences to rub together.'

I stood up feeling excited, feeling elated. I said:

'I'm going to write to my father.'

Dear Dad and Marjorie,

By the time you get this, I shall be in Paris. A friend of Alice's Aunt Daphne, who lives there, needs someone to take care of her studio for a couple of weeks, so Megan and I and another friend from Egerton Hall (Marion Tipton) will be staying there and looking after things. I'm delighted because I can consolidate my spoken French before the University entrance exams next term. This is the address: 4 Rue du Texel, Paris 14ième, France. I shall telephone if I can, though I don't know how easy it'll be, and if you could possibly see your way to sending me a cheque of the plumpish variety *by return* I'd be very grateful.

Lots of love,
Bella

I phoned Megan that night to say goodbye. I knew she couldn't come to Paris with me, because she'd already arranged to go to Scotland with Dorothy, but Marjorie needn't know that. Having Megan as part of the trip would give it, in their minds, the stamp of respectability. Safety.

'Write to me,' Megan said on the phone. 'Write to me every single day.'

'What about plunging myself into Parisian life?'

'Plunge first,' Megan laughed, 'and write later!'

Paris

Paris *the something of August, 1962*

To my dear Megan, roaming in the Scottish gloaming, *Hoots mon* and other appropriately Caledonian greetings! I have this image in my mind of you and Dorothy, standing on top of a high mountain (purple) gazing at some lochs (steel grey) in the distance. There are even, I think, some deer around. I expect the truth is she's dragging you to every stately home, art gallery and place of historical interest within miles.

I, on the other hand, am seeing a Paris far removed from the well-beaten tourist track. Not for us the Eiffel Tower, the Louvre, Les Invalides, etc. Where we are, you'd hardly know they existed. We are on the Left Bank, living La Vie Bohème with a vengeance and the most exciting thing I've seen is the back of someone who might have been Jean-Paul Sartre, the famous Existentialist Philosopher, and then again, might have been Just Anyone. I shall never know, but he was taking coffee at the Deux Magots, and he did look quite lugubrious and philosophical. I asked Greg and Phil, who were with me at the time. Phil wasn't sure if it was Sartre, and Greg wasn't sure he knew who Sartre was anyway.

I know you wanted lots of stories about my thrilling Parisian adventures, but it's been very quiet so far. I wouldn't say boring, because Paris is far too beautiful ever to be that. Really, every street corner looks like an Impressionist painting. Alice would love it. I think of her a lot, because thinking is one thing I do do plenty of, mainly in cafés. That's where I'm writing this, as a matter of fact, both because at the studio there is no clean surface on which to rest paper (see under studio, later on) and because sitting here in the sun and just writing the odd sentence and then looking up and watching all the people go by for a bit and then taking a sip of coffee is so wonderfully easy and leisured, I can't quite get over it. You can sit here all day long if you want to, as long as you keep buying the occasional cup of something. It's heaven. I try to remember what bells sound like, what having to get work done on time means, what teachers are . . . they all seem to belong to another life altogether. As for seeing things, well, there's not much going on in life that I can't see just by looking up from this page. Quite enough to fill a whole series of novels. Here are some examples at random:

1) A respectable woman dressed in a grey suit and navy hat, rather like Matron when she's putting on the style, knocking back the brandies as though they were medicine. She has a wedding ring on. I deduce her lover has let her down. He has found someone else, rather like
2) the American lady in bright colours, flashing teeth and diamonds at the waiters. She is on the lookout for a gigolo . . . I never believed there were such things outside stories by Somerset Maugham, but there's
3) a German couple hung about with cameras and with maps spread out in front of them on the table. They are talking earnestly. They will cover every square foot of Paris or die trying.

I could go on, but I shan't. It's as good as a theatre any day.

I am alone because the others have gone to do various

things I'd rather not do: chat to the management at Club Sortilège about our appearances, visit cathedrals, etc. or walk about for hours in this heat. Greg has said he will come and join me later and I daresay he will if he can remember the name of the café. If not, he will roll up at Rue du Texel when he's hungry, like a cat who turns up only when it's supper-time.

4 Rue du Texel . . . well, if this is what an artist's studio is like, I'm not a bit surprised that they die of consumption all over the place. It's hot now, so cholera is the more immediate danger, but the place has a glass roof and no visible heating system, so it must be hell in winter. It's not exactly heaven now, though traipsing down a little alley beside the house to an unspeakably filthy lavatory at the back must be even worse when it's cold. I refuse to describe this lavatory. All I can tell you is I am a recent convert to the chamber pot, quite a few of which we found in the studio when we arrived. We puzzled about them at first, but very rapidly discovered what a boon they were. There is also a shower that would not be featured in Homes and Gardens but we use it just the same. I close my eyes when I'm in there.

On to slightly less sordid things. The artist and his wife who have gone off to the seaside did not believe in housework. They hadn't even washed the dishes before they left. The first evening we all worked flat out to make the place fit to live in. You should have seen the band! I stood over them and made them mop and sweep and stack all the paintings neatly against the wall, and turn the mattress on the one available bed (mine, up on a little raised platform affair built above the main room) while I set to in the kitchen washing all those horrible dishes.

They, the band, divided the studio very carefully

between them, and I noticed that each instrument had its own special place. It may seem to an outsider as though these men live in total chaos, but if you look closely, it's quite clear that each one has his own territory, like a cat, and that the others respect all the boundaries.

'The sheets are full of holes!' I said to Harry, as he was helping me sort out the contents of the linen cupboard.

'Probably him and his family,' he answered, pointing to where a tiny mouse was peeping out from a hole in the skirting-board.

'How do you know,' I whispered, 'that he has a family?'

'Mice aren't often bachelors,' Harry said. 'And in France you get all sorts of reductions for large numbers of children. It's what they call *"une famille nombreuse"*.'

'Not too *nombreuse*, I hope,' I said. 'I'm not going to jump on a chair and shriek at the sight of one little creature, but I don't know that I want entire families scampering over my toes as I sleep.'

'I'll set up my drum kit and blast them,' said Harry. 'They won't know what hit them.'

After a few hours of back-breaking labour, the place looked almost normal. All the sleeping bags, lilos, etc. were lined up in the middle of the floor. There are two big, ugly, squashy sofas . . . the men are all playing Musical Beds so that everyone gets a turn. I'm the lucky one, upstairs on the only real live mattress. It is a double bed so it seemed only fair that I should offer to share it (on a strictly chaste feet-to-head basis, you understand) but everyone gallantly said they were fine, and they were not in Paris to sleep, but to burn the candle at both ends, etc. etc. and that thank you, yes, they would avail them-selves of my bed in groups of two or three for little naps when I was out in cafés and so on. It wouldn't surprise me if a couple of them weren't there now, having a short siesta.

Up in your Scottish fastness of clean linen and high moral tone, I can imagine you saying: 'Ugh! How can you bear to sleep in someone else's sheets?' I can see Alice wrinkling her nose in disgust and shuddering delicately. She would, I know, sit up all night on a hard chair rather than bed down in linen someone else had been sleeping on. Well, I've learned not to be so squeamish. For one thing, I know and like all these people and they are all reasonably clean, because I remind them to shower. For another I'm so intensely grateful that this bed is free of bugs and other creepy-crawlies that grubby sheets are as nothing to me. Thirdly I'm usually too tired to care about anything when I fall into my bed at dawn. Did I forget to mention that? It's very important. We don't get to see the morning, and most of the afternoon has gone by the time we get up for breakfast. This is because we are on so late at Club Sortilège. It's a bit like being on the night shift.

But the nights here are magnificent. I never realized there were so many different kinds of light. Perhaps that's why Paris is called 'La Ville Lumière'. The best light of all is in cafés at night, around lamps which seem to shine yellow. You can almost see the brush strokes fanning out all around each one, just in the way Van Gogh painted them. Out in the streets there are the neon lights of course, and lots of them are pink or green or blue and turn themselves on and off in a beautiful dance-like sequence. Then there are the headlights and tail-lights of all the cars whizzing around at high speeds, the warm light that spills on to the pavements through the café windows, and the chilly light shining out of shops closed up till the morning. The only light that fails to come up to scratch is our light in the studio. It's about sixty watts and very depressing. Luckily, we're hardly ever there at night.

It's nearly time to repair to our favourite restaurant 'A la Chaumière' for what most people think of as supper, but what I suppose is a kind of lunch for us in this topsy-turvy existence.

A bientôt, as they say over here,
Bella

*

A few days later on in August, 1962

Dear Megan,

Another dispatch from the City of Light! Life at 4 Rue du Texel has settled down to a nice routine, but Greg is looking sulkier and sulkier. This is because (he says) he has less and less time alone with me. I try to point out that living in bunches of seven (or eight if you include me), is not conducive to privacy, and that we are sort of alone for part of the evening, on our money-making venture.

Greg and I have started busking round the cafés in the early evening and very lucrative it is too. He plays the guitar and I sing all sorts of songs and then we pass round a hat. We go to big cafés like the Dôme and the Coupole and all the tourists think we're terrific and fill our hat with notes and coins. This means that we can (all eight of us) afford a slap-up meal with wine each night before we go off to the club at about midnight. Any spare cash gets divided up between Greg and me, and yes, I *will* afford a cake one day. Meanwhile, it's good fun and you see some funny things. Guess who I saw the other night? I'm sure it was her. The Dreaded Violette! – Alice's sinister great aunt. I'd recognize those eyes anywhere. She was right at the back of the café, hidden in the shadows, all draped in rusty black floaty bits and pieces, but those eyes shone out like a beacon. I don't know if she remembered me from Alice's party. In any case, I noticed it was coins and not a note she put into the hat. I daresay she's not all that wealthy. The man she was with (her husband, could it be?) was a scraggy, bearded creature dressed in shades of brown. They had a chessboard set up between them. He was concentrating on the game and she wasn't. She was moving her head this way and that, raking the half-darkness with those eyes, for all the world like a lighthouse shining out across the water, turning and turning. I'm sure it was her.

So that's the routine. We sing for our supper among the well-heeled tourists, then we have our supper, then we go along to Club Sortilège and sing all over again, for our breakfast, I suppose you could say, but it's not much money and there are eight of us.

The really blissful part about it all is the singing. I've never done so much of it in my life, and quite honestly, Megan, I feel so wonderful while I'm doing it that I wish there were a way I could go on and on doing it for ever and never stopping. The way it makes me feel is impossible to describe. The music swells up somewhere in your head (but also partly in your stomach) and then you open your mouth and are conscious of this tremendous noise vibrating all through your skull and pouring out of your mouth just carried along by your breath . . . oh, it's amazing! A really marvellous feeling. The great advantage it has over every other activity I can think of is that it takes up your whole attention while you're doing it. I get completely, totally absorbed. I never find myself thinking in the middle of a song: 'I wonder what's for dinner?' or 'What shall I wear tomorrow?' The song I'm singing has taken up all the available space in my mind and body. When the singing is over, it's as though I'm literally coming down to earth. Landing, after a flight that took me out of the real world.

But anyway, you do not want philosophizing or meditations on music, you want solid information, so I'll continue . . .

Club Sortilège is a funny sort of place. You could easily miss it altogether if you didn't know it was there. It's just a hole in the wall with steps going down to a cellar. There's a small neon sign saying Club Sortilège and an arrow pointing the way outside on the wall, but the electricity has failed or something so all you've got is an arrow flashing on and off in a half-hearted fashion. The Club is bang in the middle of the Red Light district and yes, there really are what Miss Clarke would call 'Ladies of the Night' in fishnet tights and skimpy blouses tottering around and leaning against the walls in extremely uncomfortable-looking high-heeled shoes. No one seems terribly interested in them. They come into the club from time to time for a drink and a rest and once they're sitting at a table and chatting and have kicked their shoes off they really look quite ordinary and tired and sad and old, some of them. Not at all glamorous or dangerous or exotic. If Alice could see them, she'd say they looked like the women Toulouse-Lautrec painted. They like coming to the club because it's very cosy and homelike. It sounds a strange thing to say about a nightclub, but it's true. I think I was hoping it would be full of wicked gangsters and their molls, but if the people who come here are part of the criminal underworld, then they're on their best behaviour on account of Monsieur and Madame de la Pompière running the place in respectable French bourgeois style as though it were their home, which I suppose in a way it is. Madame de la P. is known as Madame (logical, *n'est-çe pas?*) and is enormous. Tall, and with what everyone here refers to as a '*belle poitrine*' i.e. a bosom of positively Gargantuan proportions. They say she was once a dancer at the Folies Bergères and jiggled herself about clad in not much more than a feather or two . . . imagine! She rules the Sortilège empire (a kind of whitewashed cellar with a bar at one end and a bandstand at the other, and scattered chairs and tables in between) with a rod of iron. What she says goes and she says it very loudly and very quickly. Monsieur, her '*pauvre petit mari*' (that's what the Ladies of the Night call him when she's out of earshot, which isn't very often), seems henpecked but contented enough. He works behind the bar and listens constantly to Edith Piaf. Have you ever heard her songs, Megan? If there's such a thing as a record shop in your porridge-bespattered wilderness, get you thither at the double and listen to this *amazing* singer who is like no one else at all. Greg knows all about her. She is incredibly small and thin (query: could this be part of the attraction for Monsieur? A creature so different from Madame?) and has led the kind of unhappy life a novelist would never dare to invent: horrible childhood, drugs, alcohol, and truly ghastly men trampling all over her. And she sings about all of it – oh, it's enough to make you cry and break out all over in goosepimples. Listen to 'La Vie en Rose' and 'L'hymne à l'Amour'. If only I could sound like that. I shall buy some of her records while I'm here and you'll be able to hear them back at Egerton Hall. I imagine a Scottish record shop stocked entirely with eightsome reels and many moving renditions of 'Loch Lomond' but I'm sure that's not fair.

As well as the whitewashed cellar that makes up the club itself, there are various rather squalid little dressing-rooms-cum-lounges where the artistes can sit about while they're getting ready to perform. There's an unspeakable lavatory (question for the Oxbridge General Papers: how can a culture that has given us Racine and Baudelaire and Edith Piaf be so cavalier about the state of its lavatories? Discuss while holding a scented handkerchief to your nose) and a kind of cupboard which is home to Margot, an all-purpose maid and dresser and clearer-up of things. Luckily, Margot doesn't come out of her lair too often. She gives me the creeps, I can't think why. She's always quite kind, but there's a mothlike softness and wispiness about her that I can't stand, as though she might crumble if you touch her. Maybe it's her clothes. They're wafty and grey and grubby and drift about like wings. Also, she reminds me of someone I don't wish to be reminded of: that awful Em who gave me the pink suede belt in London. The resemblance is so strong that I actually asked Margot if she had relations in England. She just looked vague, so I shut up and now I try to keep out of her way as much as possible which is hard because she feels she has to help me dress. Madame herself decided on the very first night that I was not eye-catching enough. Perhaps she had a point. I was in black from head to toe, in best Parisian Existentialist style, complete with my hair hanging over my face, white lipstick and thick black eyeliner.

'*Mais c'est affreux!*' said Madame when she saw me and I have to concede she may have been right. She dragged me off to her private room and began flinging open drawers and cupboard doors, and in the twinkling of an eye every available surface was heaped with ostrich feathers, spangles, sequins, satins, laces, frills, flounces, lamé, brocade and all in blistering colours like cerise and peacock blue.

'It is necessary absolutely,' said Madame (I'm translating, of course), 'to make the dazzling impression.'

'Yes,' I said. What else could I say? I'm a great one for dazzling impressions myself, as you know, but sequins and feathers? I really didn't quite see how I was going to escape, but at last, after trying on outfit after outfit of the utmost hideousness, I found something I liked and which I now wear on stage every night. It's a dress, which already puts it way ahead of some of the things I tried, e.g. little skirt and bra sets, and things with no skirt at all at the front and a very long train affair at the back. The dress is red taffeta, low cut and very tight over the bust showing every inch of my '*belle poitrine*' with frills around the neckline. It keeps on being tight right down to my hips and then it breaks out in a sort of mad rush of flounces down to below the knee.

'It has the air,' said Madame, 'completely Spanish.' I know exactly what she meant. I could have gone straight on stage as Carmen. All I needed was a black mantilla on my hair and a rose clutched between my teeth and I'd have been ready for a Fandango. But I liked the way I looked, so I thanked Madame profusely and worried privately that perhaps the band would refuse to play with me dressed as I was. But no, they were enchanted, and made me turn around so that they could all admire me.

'That dress,' said Harry, 'could knock a chap's eyes out at twenty paces!'

'Phew! What a scorcher!' said Kenny and everyone else

whistled. Not Greg, though. He was miserable, I could see. He didn't say anything about it then, but I cornered him afterwards and he admitted it. He didn't like me looking so good for fear someone else would run off with me! I managed to convince him that the Red Dress bore no resemblance to the magical Red Shoes which made the poor girl in the story dance until she dropped down dead. I told him I was still me, and all the scarlet flounces in the world wouldn't turn me suddenly into a lustful and debauched creature, so he should stop worrying. Aren't men silly? It's true that the set went very well that night, so Madame clearly knows her stuff. I can't believe, though, that she *ever* fitted into my dress, even a hundred years ago.

Till next time,
Yours dazzlingly,
Bella

*

Paris, *later in August '62*

Oh, Megan, Megan, something awful has happened and something wonderful! Or maybe it hasn't happened. Do I sound totally mad? I feel mad. For the first time in my life I can understand *why* people want to write poems etc. and string together all the most wonderful and resplendent words they can find. It's all to do with *LOVE*. Oh, Megan, I've found it! I've found it! I know what it feels like now and I always will, but I can't ever have it . . . oh, I could cry and scream and tear my clothes, I feel so miserable. And yet I'm happy because I know what it feels like at last. I'm making very little sense. I realize that. I shall take a deep breath and make myself as calm as I possibly can and tell you the whole story, from the beginning.

I have to say one thing before I start. I've never been a believer in all this Dante and Beatrice stuff. I've had no time for stories about people who just glimpse someone once on a bridge or something – isn't that where Dante saw his beloved? – and are in thrall to them for ever, without so much as a word being spoken. It's always struck me as a lot of Romantic poppycock, thought up by male poets of the lyrical tendency. That's what I thought before this morning. Now I'm here to tell you that Dante and his ilk knew what they were talking about, and in fact may not have put the case quite strongly enough. I know this, because I have undergone just such an experience, and I don't think I'll ever recover.

This is what happened. I'm terrified to write it down in case it's like a dream and just putting it into words robs it of some of its magic.

Last night, from about ten o'clock, the Sortilège was very crowded. There was a party in from the Sorbonne: foreign students, most of them, who had come over to Paris for a spot of French language and culture during the summer hols. Lots of them were American. You could tell at once – I don't quite know how. Perhaps it was their height or their clothes, or their very good teeth, or it might have been something to do with their loud exclamations about everything in American accents. I caught gems like: 'Gee, they have a band here . . . let's stay and hear how they sound . . .' from where I was sitting, near the bar, and I felt irritated. It was as if they were willing us to be not-so-hot, saying to us: impress us if you can. We're from the kingdom of Jazz, Elvis country, Buddy Holly land.

'Don't flare your nostrils like that, Bella,' Greg said. 'We'll show them. We'll do "Suitcase". That'll sort them out.'

I laughed. 'Suitcase' is an amazingly fast, jazzy, upbeat number that takes every scrap of energy and breath in my body. I also sing it very loudly, so that it just about takes the roof off the room I'm doing it in.

'Is the Sortilège built for it, I wonder? Won't the place just cave in?'

'Let's risk it,' said Greg, 'and then we'll follow up with "Sleeping" to calm them down.'

So that's what we did when it came to my set. I blasted them with a few gentle verses of 'Suitcase':

> Look at this suitcase, full of stuff
> does it look like a heart to you?
> Let me tell you, enough's enough
> and I'm unpacking, baby, it's true.
> Out they go
> the hugs and kisses
> dates and wishes
> promises and I love you,
> photographs
> and lots of laughs
> and memories
> that make me blue
> all your cheating
> all your lying
> all my sighing
> and my crying –
> from now on
> I'm butterflying!
> Out goes loving

turtledoveing
I'll go jazzing
razzmatazzing.
I'm tossing out
the things you gave me
the necklaces
and rings you gave me
taking off
the wings you gave me
when we flew
when love was new –
Baby, I'm grounded now
yessir.
Baby, I'm grounded now.

The song goes on in this vein for three minutes with Harry doing his utmost on the drums. You can imagine the effect. Just as I was taking a bow (and I have to hand it to the American contingent. They were very enthusiastic applauders) I glanced towards the steps leading down from outside and I saw him. I couldn't stop looking at him, Megan, because he was the most beautiful person I had ever seen in my life: tall and dark and with eyes the colour of aquamarines. He came to sit at a table quite near the front, and I heard everyone say: 'Hi, Mark!' and 'Look, Mark's here!' and so I knew his name. I just gazed and gazed at him, until Greg said:

'Bella, what's the matter? What's wrong? Aren't we going to do "Sleeping"?'

'Yes,' I whispered. 'Yes, we'll do it.' My mouth was dry, and I could hear my heart beating in the very centre of my head, louder than the drumbeat. I started to sing, and I sang it for him, for Mark. The spotlight grew smaller and smaller until I could sense it on my face, and the rest of the club was in semi-darkness. As I sang the words, I could feel them flying up out of my mouth and into the air and wrapping themselves around this man, this Mark, like a caress. Oh, I meant every one of them, Megan.

My eyes were closed
before I looked at you.
I was asleep
when you came in.
Then there you were
and when I looked at you
the world inside my heart
began to spin.
My heart was ice
before you melted it.
I was asleep
and feeling blue.
Now here you are
and when you look at me
the sweetest dreams I have
are filled with you.

Don't you think it's significant, that we should have decided to sing just that song and at just that moment? It seems to me as if it was Meant, part of some great plan, although I know you'll probably be giggling at such a far-fetched suggestion. Anyway, I sang, and as I did, I knew Mark's eyes were on me, and when the song was finished and the lights came on again, I met his gaze and didn't look away. Not for a long time. The look just stretched out between us like a thin, silver wire, vibrating, quivering, and I could feel him drinking me in, every bit of me, consuming me there where I stood, scanning my face as though he had to learn it quickly, immediately: learn it by heart to keep it for ever. I looked back at him, until Greg said:

'Right, Bella, that was great. Come and have a drink.' He took my hand and led me over to a table far away from the one Mark was at. I could feel the disappointment rising in me, making me feel sick. I wanted to tear my hand out of Greg's and run to the table down by the dance floor and sit next to Mark. You're being stupid, I said to myself. He's with a whole gang of his friends. You can't go barging in there. Maybe one of those fresh-faced, sparkly-looking young women is his girlfriend. He was only looking at you like that because he liked the way you sing. Lots of people like the way you sing. It doesn't mean anything really. It's just a kind of spell that is broken as the last note of the music dies away, that's all. You can imagine what kind of gloomy thoughts I was having, Megan, without me telling you. Then, I noticed a flurry of chair-scraping and goodbyes being called out and I saw that Mark's party was leaving. I couldn't bear it. They were going . . . he was going and I'd never see him again. He actually began to make his way up the steps when quite suddenly he turned and came back to where I was sitting with the others. I think it was the force of my longing directed at his back that made him return, made him come and speak to me. He said:

'Excuse me, Miss, but could I have a word with you?' I was too overcome to speak. I nodded and stood up and we walked over to a corner near the staircase.

'I just wanted,' he began, and hesitated. 'I just wanted to say how much I enjoyed your singing. It was terrific.'

'Thank you,' I said.

He shook his head. 'No, I don't just want to say that. That sounds as lame as hell. I'm sorry. I don't know what to say, and that's the truth. I'm leaving Paris on the six a.m. flight tomorrow and I'll be back in Medical School in Boston in a couple of weeks. Otherwise . . .' He let the word hang in the air.

'Otherwise what?' I said.

'Never mind,' he said. 'Only I want you to know . . .' he looked around as if searching for the right words, 'that I'll always remember you. Always.'

I blushed. I said, 'I don't even know your name.'

'Mark. Mark Eschen. I have to go now . . . they'll be back and drag me off if I don't.'

'Okay,' I said. ''Bye.'

''Bye,' he whispered and ran up the steps. At the top, he looked back and it seemed to me as though he made some kind of movement that might have been a kiss. I think he made the shape of a kiss with his mouth. I groaned, because the pain I felt, the loss I felt, was so terrible. He was here, with me, within my grasp and I'd let him go. He doesn't even know my name, I thought. He knows nothing about me, nothing about where to find me. I should have gone with him, jumped on the flight to Boston, not let him out of my sight. As it is, all I have to remember him by are his name and the memory of his eyes on my face, and a half-blown kiss in the dark that may not have been a kiss at all.

I went back to where the others were chatting and sat down in a daze. Greg was looking sad and sulky.

'What've you done with your Stage-door Johnnie, Bella?' Phil said. 'He was properly smitten, wasn't he?'

'He's going back to America tomorrow,' I said. This had a remarkable effect on Greg. It was as though a cloud had floated past the sun. He started smiling at everyone and immediately put an arm around my shoulders. I hardly noticed. You can't be sad at losing him, I said to myself. You've only exchanged a couple of sentences with him. You don't know him. But 'sad' wasn't the word for what I felt. It was more as though I'd been struck by lightning. I felt shaken. I felt as though I would never be myself properly again. I had loved him. That was what had happened to me. Only for a few minutes, it's true, but oh, Megan, with such intensity, such longing! Of course I realize that I will probably never see him again, so that's that.

There you are. Not much of a story, is it? But my dreams are so full of him, Megan, and because I've never really known him, I can make him into whatever I choose. I sing every song for him now. Greg says, 'You're singing better than ever,' and I feel so guilty! Poor Greg! What shall I tell him? I think I'll have to tell him the truth eventually, but I don't want to hurt him and I will. Who invented love, Megan? Didn't they make a dreadful *mess* of it? Why can it almost never be all right? Oh, I could weep! Pay no attention to me. I'm raving and incoherent. I'm sure you remember what it's like. Perhaps next time I write, I'll feel a little more normal.

Tons of love,
Bella

*

Paris, *Summer '62 etc.*

Dear old Megan,

A couple of days have passed and although the first delirious babblings have subsided somewhat, both in my breast and (it is to be hoped) on paper, I am still haunted by the knowledge that somewhere in the world Mark – isn't it a wonderful name? – is walking around, alive. I see his face in dreams and my thoughts turn to him quite a lot, but I shan't bore you with that. Unless something exciting is happening in any romance, I do think people should keep quiet, don't you? All that pure undiluted feeling and yearning is terribly tedious for everyone else. So as I've nothing more to report on that front, I'll go on to other things.

Club Sortilège is as usual. I'm getting quite attached to the old place. A white cat has adopted us. One of the Night Ladies must have fed it or something and now it hangs around the stage door, and occasionally even comes in and takes up residence in one of the dressing-rooms. This is okay, except if Margot finds it. She doesn't like cats at all, and flicks at it with a duster, and hisses at it and the poor creature runs for its life and skulks behind the dust-bins outside. Why do all the cats I see look like poor Snowflake? Is it that they're the only ones that catch my eye? It's mysterious and that's a fact.

There's not really very much news. Life at the studio is okay. We are just about keeping our heads above the surface of the chaos. I'm not sure what I'm doing wrong. Perhaps eight people is more than the place can take, but it is very hard to keep it looking decent. Things do lie about so, and if you're not careful, they'll engulf you. That's what it seems like to me. And in spite of the fact that I do hardly any cooking at all, there's always stacks of washing-up. Another mystery; life is full of them.

People like my singing, so that makes me happy. We are *un succès fou* at the Sortilège and I have to do encores every night. Madame thinks it's the red dress and I'm sure she's right.

I'm not feeling myself today, Megan, and it's because of a quarrel I've had with Greg. It happened the night after I'd seen Mark, so I suppose my nerves were jangling, or something. At least that's my excuse, but I should never have . . . well, let me start at the beginning. Greg was pestering me, asking me what was wrong . . . why was I different . . . what had he done, etc. etc. I tried to say nothing. I pleaded tiredness, but he went on and on. In the end, I couldn't bear it another moment. I said:

'I'm sorry, Greg, I'm sorry to have to tell you this, but I'm in love with someone else.'

As soon as the words were out of my mouth, I wished I hadn't said them. Poor Greg looked stunned, wounded. He said:

'You can't be. You haven't . . . where did you meet him?'

'Last night at the club.'

'That guy?' (He relaxed a bit.) 'I saw you both . . . you only talked to him for about three minutes and then he was gone. How can you be in love with someone you hardly know?'

'Oh, I know all I need to know about him,' I said.

'I don't believe it.' Greg laughed. 'You're not letting me anywhere near you because of someone who just happened to be there last night while you sang?'

'It wouldn't be fair to you,' I said. 'Leading you on when I don't really love you.'

Oh, Megan, I said it, and he looked . . . he looked as though all the separate bits of his face were going to disintegrate.

'You don't love me,' he whispered. 'I thought . . .'

I tried to backtrack. I tried to make it better and only

made it worse. I muttered about different kinds of love, and always being his friend and loving his music. I chattered on and while I was chattering, Greg, I could see, was just smouldering, getting angrier and angrier every moment. We were the only ones in the studio and we were in the kitchen. I'd actually persuaded Greg to help me with the washing-up, which meant he had all the ammunition ready to hand for when he lost his temper. I didn't realize he was losing it until it was thoroughly lost, if you see what I mean. He started very quietly, muttering into the dirty water and then got louder and louder until by the end he was yelling at me:

'Jesus, Bella, I don't know what you want. I mean, what else was I supposed to do? I thought, when you first came to the house, I thought you liked me. You *did* like me. You said you did and you bloody well behaved as though you did, or have you conveniently forgotten that, eh?' He turned round and snarled at me. 'I think . . . you know what I think? I think you've lost your mind, that's what. I don't think it's true, any of that stuff you said, because I think you *do* love me, and the rest of that waffle, all the bit about the mystery man at the Sortilège is just made up, rubbish, total *bullshit*! You sing my songs as though you mean them, don't you?' His voice subsided a bit at this point.

'Of course I mean it,' I said. 'I love your songs, you know I do. Don't you know that?'

'Well, that proves it then. Those songs are me. The best bits of me. If you love them, you love me. It's logical.'

'It's not a bit logical. I admire you, of course, for being able to write the songs, but it doesn't follow at all that I love you. Oh, Greg, I'm only trying to be honest with you.'

This was when he saw red. He actually picked up cups and saucers from the draining board and started flinging them round the room.

'Who the hell asked you to be honest, eh? Who gave you the right to go tearing into people with all this truth?' I didn't answer. I was cowering behind a chair. Greg shook his head and looked around him as though he'd suddenly come out of a dream.

'Oh, God,' he said, 'look what I've done now.'

He started going round the floor of the studio picking up the pieces of broken china and tears were just pouring down his face.

I said, 'Greg, don't cry. I can't bear it. It's better if you yell at me.'

'I can't help it,' he said. 'I can't stop.'

'Please, Greg,' I said, crying myself now. 'Please stop. I don't mean to hurt you, but I can't lie to you and I can't help what I feel.'

I sat down at the kitchen table and began to cry as I haven't cried since I was a small child. I bawled. I howled. I sobbed. I screamed. And the tears just poured and poured out of me. As I cried, I could feel that I was weeping about everything: everything I'd never properly wept about all through my life: I cried for sorrow for Alice and for anger at that animal who hurt her and I cried for the loss of my cat who'd been killed and I think for the first time in my life I even cried for my mother. And of course, Greg tried to stop me, and I pushed him away and said:

'Let me cry. It's good for me to cry.'

'But how are you going to be able to sing tonight? Your eyes'll be like two slices of boiled beetroot.'

That made me laugh in the midst of my tears. Greg found a bottle of wine and poured us a drink.

'What do my eyes look like?' he asked. 'Men aren't supposed to cry.'

'You shouldn't cry for me,' I said. 'I'm not worth the tears.'

'You are,' said Greg, 'to me.'

'I'm really sorry,' I said, hiccuping from the after-effects of all those tears. 'I really am. I didn't mean to hurt you.'

'Never mind,' said Greg. 'I'll get over it by the time I'm forty, I expect. But I still can't believe what you told me. About that bloke last night at the Sortilège. Is it true?'

'Yes,' I said, 'it's true, and that's the last time I'm ever going to see him.' I started crying again.

'Bloody hell, Bella,' said Greg, 'don't begin all over again or we'll all drown!'

I stopped in the end. Well, you have to, don't you? The show has to go on, doesn't it? Thank heavens for eye make-up, that's what I say, and for Madame's red dress, which, as they say in all the best fashion magazines, 'attracts the eye towards the bust line'. Fortunately my breasts are not transparent, or the entire clientele of the Sortilège would have been able to gaze at my bruised and bleeding heart.

Yours, expiring in a Paris studio
from impossible dreams of love,
   Bohemian Bella

*

August 25th, 1962

Dear Megan,

I know that people say 'I wish you were here' all the time, but I really mean it, and really do wish it, and the thought that I won't see you until almost the beginning of next term is truly ghastly. I need you. I need to tell you things. So much has happened and it would be such a relief to have you to discuss it with. As it is, I have to limit myself to this rather inadequate means of communication. That is the one thing – the only thing – I am looking forward to next term: chatting to you again. I *think* I'm dreading the thought of going back to Egerton Hall, but that may well be because since arriving here the whole of my normal life seems to have no more reality than the painted backdrop of a pantomime seen long ago. I blame all this foreign travel. I am not myself. Even these long letters aren't like me, are they? But there's such a lot I want to tell you . . . two things mainly. So here goes.

Our time here is almost at an end. I feel nostalgic about this café, and this table, even before I've left it. I also have the impression that everything has changed and become steadily darker since I first wrote to you. It was only two weeks ago, and already the letters I wrote then seem to belong to another life and to have been written by a 'me' who was altogether bouncier and more optimistic. I think I must be still not quite over what happened on Thursday night, the day before yesterday. The doctor at the hospital who put the stitches in said that I was lucky to avoid blood-poisoning. Don't be alarmed, Megan. I'm telling this the wrong way round. I'm okay really, but my energy has been sapped and I don't seem to have my usual enthusiasm. Oh, things are different!

The truth of the matter is, ever since seeing Mark and having the row with Greg, I've been in a foul temper. I am impatient with everyone because nothing seems worth doing any more. It scarcely seems worth walking around in a world without Mark in it – no, don't worry, I'm not in the least suicidal, just furious that a certain combination of features should have brought me to this *silly and undignified pass*. I'm livid with myself. I hate the sort of person I've become: given to weeping for no good reason, and fantasizing my way through some of the daylight hours and most of the night-time ones.

I was a little unnerved on Thursday night even before we got to the Sortilège. This was because I had seen the dreaded Violette again, and this time there was no mistake. She actually spoke to me. Greg and I had been busking. I was taking the hat round. I hadn't noticed her, right at the back of the café, all by herself.

'You don't remember me,' she said, in that terrible, rusty voice. 'I'm Alice's Aunt Violette.'

I looked at her properly then. That was a bit of a shock as well. When we saw her at Alice's party she must have been all done up. She looked quite different now, all thin and pinched and white in the face, and oh, Megan, so dreadfully old! The skin round her mouth was puckered into lines, there were hundreds of wrinkles round her eyes and her neck was leathery and scraggy like a chicken's. Her eyes blazed at me. I found I had to turn away. She put a hand on my arm while she was talking. It looked like a claw, or the talon of a bird. The nails were painted such a dark red that they seemed almost black.

'Of course I remember you,' I said and smiled my most charming smile. 'We met recently at Alice's party.'

'Alice . . .' said Violette. 'How is Alice now?' I wondered briefly who had told her about Alice and how much she knew. I decided she couldn't know everything, so I said:

'She's a lot better now, I believe. The doctors are very pleased with her progress.'

'Really?' Violette looked at me and frowned. 'That's not

what I heard at all.' She stood up, towering above me, gathering the folds of her robe or cloak or whatever it was closer about her. Then she leaned down and whispered in my ear:

'I hear she's knocking,' (she rapped with a bony, ring-encrusted hand on the marble tabletop), 'knocking at Death's Door.' She laughed a hideous laugh, and wound her way between the tables, waving goodbye to me as she went with her skeletal fingers, a kind of death's-head grin on her face.

I made Greg buy me a drink after that. I was shaken and upset, and couldn't help worrying about Alice. She *will* be all right, Megan, won't she? I really couldn't bear it if she isn't.

Anyway, you can imagine that after such an encounter I wasn't in the best of moods. Thursday night, our second-to-last performance (and my last, although I didn't know it then), had been talked about for days. It was to be a Gala. All this meant was that the Ladies of the Night were encouraged to drag their gentlemen friends in, Monsieur and Madame invited every elderly reprobate they could think of (and assured us that some of them were real live music critics), drinks were more expensive than usual, the floor had been swept, and Madame herself was the centre of attention in diamanté-studded grey satin, like a sea lion ready for a Hunt Ball. It had also been decided, before I arrived in my less-than-Gala mood, that a special effort was to be made to improve on the red, flouncy dress. Madame herself came into my little dressing-room to tell me her decision. She was herding poor Margot into the room ahead of her, as if she were a small child who need-ed to be told where to go. Margot was in her habitual moth-grey bits and pieces, Gala or no Gala.

'Sit yourself there, *chérie*,' Madame said to her, and then turned to me. 'You are going certainly to excuse me for interrupting you,' she began.

'But naturally,' I said, trying hard to smile.

'I have been considering what one must do to give you the air Gala . . .' I nodded and hmmed non-committally. '. . . and at first I thought that it would be a question of the addition of a few jewels, simply . . .' (oh, well, I was thinking, if it'll please the old bat, I'll doll myself up in a couple of strands of glass beads . . . why not?) '. . . but then I decided that that would not walk well at all . . .' (please remember I am translating exactly from the French!). 'One has need, I think, of a coiffure.'

I knew what she meant by that. I didn't need a translation and neither will you. We both know that a coiffure is to a hairdo what champagne is to Lucozade, and that what Madame had in mind was the kind of arrangement it takes about half an hour to create. I said:

'But I haven't the time for a coiffure, and besides, it's ten o'clock at night. All the salons have been closed for hours.'

A look of triumph which would not have disgraced Napoleon at Austerlitz crossed Madame's face.

'But it is for this that I bring Margot!' She leaned towards me, and the whalebones in her corset could be heard creaking. 'Margot, who has only been working here for a few weeks, is nevertheless known to me as a veritable artiste of the hair. She will transform you . . . you must believe me.'

'Oh, I do, I do! But surely it will be a lot of trouble . . . surely I could just put it up like this . . .' I indicated a French pleat with my hands. I hated the thought of those pallid fingers fluttering round in my hair. Margot, too, it has to be said, was sitting in her chair looking distinctly unkeen on the whole idea.

'No, no,' Madame said, in a tone which signalled the interview was nearly over. 'Absolutely not. Margot will create you here a masterpiece.' And as though to silence any further reservations I might have had, she produced her trump card. Turning to Margot, she said:

'Show her the comb. She will not be able to resist.'

She smiled at us both and swept out of the room. Margot was scrabbling about, meanwhile, in the folds of her skirt. Then she stood up and came to stand behind me, so that I could see her in the rather spotty mirror. It's typical of Club Sortilège that they have light bulbs all round the mirror in best Hollywood style, and only half of them are actually working. It's enough light to see by and not enough to be cruel: an ideal arrangement. Margot held up what was in her hand, and showed it to me in the mirror. I gasped. The comb was thickly encrusted with obviously false but still blindingly twinkling gems in all the colours of the rainbow. The whole thing should have been hideous, but was curiously attractive. I can't explain why, but all of a sudden I wanted nothing more than an elaborate structure on the top of my head, anchored into place with that magnificent comb. I could just see myself under the follow-spot, with the comb bouncing tiny arrows of coloured light into the dark corners of the cellar.

'It's lovely!' I said to Margot, trying to be friendly, trying to inject some kind of warmth into my voice. Was I going to have to chat to her? I cringed at the thought. Whatever could I say? I'd never found it difficult to talk to Armand. He was always so ready with delightfully appetizing morsels of society gossip, and, of course, we used to discuss Marjorie at great length. Fortunately it became clear as Margot began to comb and pin my hair that she, too, preferred to work in silence. I watched as the coiffure began to take shape, thinking how vulnerable I felt. This person I hardly knew had the power to transform me. She could make me beautiful, but she could also, if the whim came upon her, put her hands into the recesses of her garments and pull out some scissors and cut every bit of my hair off. She could make me hideous. For a moment I felt a tremor of fear, but the sight of her, heaping one curl on the next so carefully and daintily, was strangely hypnotic. For a second, I felt my eyelids droop, but I was woken, brought to myself again, when Margot spoke.

'Now,' she said, 'we must fasten the comb. It will feel a little tight at first, but do not worry. It is for the security, you understand. So that it should not fall.'

She pushed the comb into my hair, driving the teeth through the spirals and loops she had fashioned, and twisting it a little before pushing it into position. I winced at the pain. It felt as if all the hairs around the teeth of the comb had been pulled too tight. After a bit, I thought, I'll get used to it. I smiled at Margot in the mirror and said:

'Thank you so much. It looks very nice. Very Gala.'

Margot simply nodded and gave a half-smile and then left. I looked at myself more carefully in the mirror. Even in this dim light, the jewels on the comb shone with a heart-lifting radiance. All of a sudden I felt strangely elated. Even the thought that I might never see Mark again seemed to be romantic rather than depressing. I was slightly dizzy, as well. Perhaps I should have eaten something with the drink Greg had bought me earlier in the evening. I should send someone out to get a sandwich. As soon as I thought that, I felt sick. Then the sickness passed and I felt weak. Straight after the show tonight, I promised myself, I shall go to sleep and not wake up until I'm quite rested. What the Club Sortilège needed, I decided, was someone like Matron. She'd make sure that all the artistes kept sensible hours and didn't let themselves get run down. I smiled to think what Matron would say if she could see me dressed like this, ready to go on and sing in front of a whole lot of strangers in a Paris basement.

Just then, Greg stuck his head round the door and said: 'We're on,' and I stood up.

What happened next, the whole sequence of events from the time I went on stage (Thursday midnight) until about lunchtime on Friday is like a dream. Some parts are clear and sharp. They stand out in my mind like pictures hung on a white, white wall. Some of them do not make sense, but they are vivid, brightly coloured. All the rest is space: misty and white, and in the space sometimes I can hear voices, and sometimes the voices blur and become thick and unclear.

Mainly, I remember the pain. As I sang the first couple of songs, it seemed as though the whole room was moving further and further away from me. Even the people at the tables right beside the stage looked as though they were at the wrong end of a telescope. I could sense the light pouring out from the jewels in my comb, but instead of dazzling the audience, I felt as if it was burning small holes in my scalp, and that the teeth of the comb were embedding themselves deeper and deeper in my head . . . they will go down and down, I thought fuzzily, and bore right through my scalp and through my skull and into the soft parts of my brain. That was the last thought I can recall with any certainty, and then a great wave of blackness broke over my head.

The next clear picture is of looking down at my hand,

lying on a red blanket. My hand is being stroked by Greg's. There is a bright line of light moving across a window. I've been told by Greg that Madame sent immediately for an ambulance, the moment I collapsed on to the stage.

'What happened to the comb?' I asked Greg today.

'I don't know. I suppose it must have fallen out somewhere. We were all too worried about you to bother about it. The doctor wanted to see it, after you'd told them you had holes in your head . . . but it was too late by then. The Sortilège would have been closed.'

That's another picture: the doctor frowning at me. Pressing his lips together and shaking his head. They had to shave a tiny bit of hair off, Megan. Luckily, no one can see it, because I can comb the rest of my hair to cover it up and of course it will grow back. Still, sometimes I imagine the small patch of shaved scalp to be as wide as a desert, and those pinpricks that caused me so much pain looking like wells brimming with blood.

'This comb,' I remember the doctor asking me, 'could it have been contaminated? Poisoned? Do you know where it was kept before it was used in your hair?'

I shook my head then. Later I asked Greg:

'Why did he mention poison?' and Greg said:

'Apparently, your reaction was very extreme. Not what he would have expected, he said, from what was after all quite a superficial injury.'

I came back to the studio to rest. The doctor absolutely forbade me to go on stage last night for the final performance. I was quite relieved. Greg said:

'I'll stay with her. You can manage without me, too.'

'But what about the paying customers?' said Pete. 'It's bad enough that Bella's off without losing you as well.'

'Yes,' I said, feeling better by now. 'Pete's right. You ought to go.'

Greg looked stubborn and said quite harshly:

'I don't give a tuppenny damn about the paying customers. I'm staying here and looking after Bella, and if you don't like it, tough.'

'Okay,' Pete said, clearly taken aback by Greg's uncharacteristically firm statement. 'It's okay. It can't be helped. I'll explain . . . to everyone. Any messages, Bella?'

'Say goodbye for me,' I said.

When the others came back after the last performance in the early hours of Saturday morning, Greg and I were already asleep. They'd arranged the dress over the back of the chair, so that it was the first thing I saw when I woke up.

'Madame said you should keep it,' said Phil. 'She actually made a joke. She said it no longer fitted her, and until she got her figure back, the dress was yours. Don't you reckon that counts as a joke?'

I did. I was very touched, and burst into tears to think of Madame's kindness. Then I remembered the comb. I said:

'Did anyone find the comb?' and they all shook their heads. Kenny said:

'I asked about that. Everyone claimed not to have seen it, but one of the Ladies . . . Lizette, is that her name? the redhead . . . told me later that she'd seen Margot throwing something small wrapped in newspaper into the outside bin. She also said she saw that white cat sniffing around there, and that Margot stamped her foot at him and he ran away.'

'Oh, well,' I said, 'good riddance to the comb, anyway.'

I haven't told Greg this, nor any of the others, but

sometimes, Megan, I wonder whether everything isn't linked together in some way. You're going to think I'm crazy, I know, but in my worst moments I can convince myself that it's Marjorie who's at the bottom of everything. Ever since she tried to lose me that time in Harrods, I think she's wanted me gone – out of her life. Sometimes I think she'd be quite pleased if I died. Do you remember how I choked on one of her apples, a couple of terms ago, and had to go to the San? Then the belt and now the comb, and also the fact that Em and Margot are so *like* Marjorie in so many ways, and the white cats I keep seeing – are they some kind of warning? Some sign? You will think I'm still delirious, I know. And I also know exactly what you'll tell me. I know all the reasonable explanations for everything. Marjorie is jealous of me. Marjorie is quite capable of trying to make my life difficult. She doesn't especially care if she doesn't see too much of me – but the rest is in my mind, a figment of my over-active imagination. Em and Margot looking like one another and like Marjorie is only a coincidence. The belt and the comb are accidents, and the cats are separate white cats, of which there are plenty in the world. They are of no special significance. It's exactly like Alice's story all over again: did what happened to Alice come about because the Dreaded Violette wished it to be so, or for other reasons? The truth is, we'll never know and our answers – my answers – depend on what time of day it is. During the bright and sunshiny daylight hours, I'm as rational as the next person, but waking from a bad dream and staring through the dark in the long hours before morning, I believe my worst fears are true. I believe everything.

So there you are, Megan. Another chapter in The Paris Adventures of an English Schoolgirl. Tomorrow night, we are coming back to England. I may manage one more letter. There is still something I have to tell you, something important. Maybe I should wait until I see you.

Enigmatically yours,
Bella

Dear Megan,

I've thought and thought (for about twenty minutes, truly! It proved to be the most tremendous effort. My poor little brain is quite rusty and out of practice) about whether I should write to you about this, or wait until I see you. In the end, as you can see, I've decided to write. My reasons are:

1) I want to get it off my chest.
2) I don't think I could find the right words if I had to tell you face to face. I'd be embarrassed.
3) There's nothing much else to do for the next few hours before the train leaves. All the others are lying about reading, playing cards, etc. and Greg is working on a new song . . . I bet I know what it'll be about, but I digress.

Okay. Here it is then. Last night I let Greg make love to me. (Oh, I *am* glad I'm writing this and not saying it! I'm blushing just from setting the words down on this piece of paper.) I feel guilty towards poor Greg for not loving him properly, completely, in the way I *know* I would be capable of loving Mark, but at least I have made him happy and I have to admit I'm not miserable either. In fact, it's done quite a lot to cheer me up and I recommend it as a cure for all kinds of ailments, including lingering pains in the head caused by stitches after an accident with a comb. It's also made me realize that I have to put Mark right out of my head and consign him to the category of Adolescent Fantasy, along with Elvis, Buddy, Marlon Brando and all the other heroes who are not real people in my mind, but almost fictional characters whom you can idolize and dream about without there being any real danger of hurting yourself. You remember I was still in a very woozy state on Friday evening. The doctor had given me some painkilling pills which not only dulled the pain but also made me feel fuzzy round the edges, like a picture that's not been coloured in terribly neatly. By about six o'clock, all the members of the band had gone out to one place or another. Phil and Harry had made some soup from a packet and left instructions with Greg about heating it up and giving it to me at regular intervals to build up my strength.

So, at about eleven o'clock, Greg said:

'I've got some soup here,' and came upstairs with a bowl in one hand and a spoon stuck into his belt. 'Phil says I'm to give it to you. Do you think he means I have to spoonfeed you?'

'No,' I said, 'I'm sure he doesn't. I think I can manage. Just help me to sit up a bit. Can you pile these pillows behind my back?'

'Okay,' said Greg. Suddenly, I was very hungry, and I started spooning the soup up quite enthusiastically.

'I feel much better now,' I said.

'Well enough to hear a song I've just written?'

I nodded again, because my mouth was full of soup. Greg ran down the rickety stairs to get his guitar. He started playing the introduction on his way up.

'I could stay and play it down there,' he said. 'Like a kind of serenade . . .'

'No, I want to hear it properly,' I said. 'I love the beat.'

And I did. Under the sheet, my feet were already tapping to the rhythm: what I always think of as a driven, pushed-through-a-saxophone-with-great-force kind of rhythm, the kind spangled dancing girls strut their stuff to, and even take their clothes off to . . . typical nightclub music.

'It's written,' said Greg, 'in honour of your red dress.'

I've got my red dress, sugar
and my high heels on
and I'm turning all the lights on
till my blues are gone.
Making that darkness
turn so bright,
I'm gonna sing my sorrows, honey
Clear out of sight.

Don't want no sad pictures
no, no, no,
don't want no
never, no, never
don't want no sad pictures,
sad pictures of the night.

Don't want no dark snaps, baby,
cos everything's all right.
Just want a lit-up set of memories
yeah
yeah
a floodlit set of memories
to bring the good times back.
In my pictures of the night,

I'm gonna lose the black.

'That's fantastic,' I said. 'That's my very favourite of all your songs. Can I learn it tomorrow?'

'Whenever you like. I'm sorry you couldn't get to sing it at the Sortilège. But there'll be other gigs, won't there? In London?'

I nodded. I didn't know how often I would see Greg and the others next term. I think they'd quite forgotten there ever were such things in the world as schools, universities, exams, etc. I didn't blame them. I'd practically forgotten myself. I just said:

'Greg, do you remember what I told you in London?'

'What's that then?'

'That I thought my stepmother tried to kill me . . . do you remember, when my belt wouldn't come off?'

Greg laughed. 'Oh, right! I'd forgotten that . . . you doing your "I am a Gothic heroine" routine. I thought you were a bit . . . I don't know . . . delirious at the time. What with fainting and everything.'

'You're going to think I'm even more delirious now then.'

'Why?'

'Because I'm sure . . . almost sure . . . that Margot meant that comb to harm me last night, and that in some way . . . don't ask me how . . . I don't know how . . . Marjorie was behind it. No, okay, I'm not going to say another word. I can see you think I've taken leave of my senses. I take it all back. Feverish babblings, that's all. Just the sickness talking.'

'I should hope so, too.' Greg looked relieved. 'That would *really* be crazy, Bella. We'd have had to send for a doctor with a Viennese accent at least three inches thick!'

I kept quiet about my suspicions after that. Of course Greg was right, and yet I couldn't shake off what I felt deep down: that in spite of the fact that there was no visible connection between Marjorie and Margot, it was Marjorie's malicious intentions guiding the whole incident.

Anyway, I decided to change the subject.

'It's ever so nice of you,' I said, 'to miss the last night at the Sortilège and stay and look after me.'

'I like looking after you,' he said and blushed. 'I'd like . . .'

'What would you like?' I grinned. I was flirting with him, Megan, I knew I was. I had a very good idea of what he would say.

'I'd like to look after you always,' he muttered, so quietly that I could hardly hear him. I put the bowl (empty now) on the floor and leaned forward to wind my arms around him. Just suddenly I was full of affection for him, felt like hugging him and stroking his hair. So I did hug him, in a cuddly sort of way, and he began to shake. That's really the only way to describe it, Megan. He was trembling, and his lips were burning hot. I could feel them on my hair and my mouth and my neck and soon, before I knew what was happening, he had undone my pyjama buttons, and had buried his face in my breasts. It's not that I wasn't enjoying all this. I don't want you to think of me as entirely cold-hearted. I liked it. I didn't care if it went on for ages and ages, but at no point did I ever lose control of myself. I mean, I even found myself wondering if Greg had ever done this with Rilly Maxton of the porky thighs. I'm sure that's not how it's meant to be, is it, Megan? I can remember quite clearly thinking: 'it's going to happen soon. I'm not going to say no. I'm going to let

Greg undress me, make love to me. I shall know how it feels'. I was taking an almost scientific interest in what was happening. Part of me seemed to be detached, watching the antics on the bed from a spot near the ceiling somewhere. I thought at one point: 'This will hurt. I'm sure it's supposed to hurt the first time' but it didn't hurt at all. Maybe that was because of all the painkillers I'd taken for my head.

I think afterwards we must have fallen asleep for ages. I woke up and Greg was still asleep next to me. I could see him quite clearly in the moonlight coming through the glass roof above my head. I touched his shoulder and his back, and it felt so soft and smooth that I was quite surprised. I don't know what I thought a man's back would be like – all hard and armour-plated like an armadillo's perhaps – but it made me feel sad all at once to think that they were just like girls in so many things, especially when they were asleep. I think in some ways they are even more vulnerable than we are. Greg cried last night, Megan. Real tears. He kept saying how happy he was and weeping and weeping. My neck and shoulder were quite damp. I felt strong by contrast. I have a kind of power over him now. I know that, and it worries me. What will become of him if I ever leave him? This thought made me feel cold in the middle of a hot August night, and immediately I began to scheme, to think of various ways in which I could distance myself. Perhaps I should say it was a mistake? I could say I wasn't feeling quite well, that we must draw a line under all this before it was too late. I fell asleep pondering these weighty matters. Then (it must have been around dawn . . . the studio was empty . . . the others must have gone to Les Halles to eat onion soup or something) Greg woke up and began kissing me again, and it was even nicer the second time. I decided not to say anything for now. Am I being utterly beastly, Megan? Am I immoral, enjoying it so much without actually being in love with the person? Oh, I wish I had you here to talk to! We will have tons of things to discuss when we meet. Till then, I should stop writing and start packing. We leave Paris in an hour. The caravan moves on!

Lots of love,
Bella

Egerton Hall

Hip, hip, hooray! We have all of us, Megan and Alice and I, passed our exams! The envelope was waiting for me when I came home from Paris. My father had prudently decided it should await my arrival, rather than surprise me while I was abroad. I was glad of it, because it distracted him from interrogating me too closely about my time in France with Megan and Marion Tipton . . . I had almost forgotten the story I had told before setting out for Paris. Anyway, I have done rather better than I expected, and almost before the envelope had been opened, the siren voices began and the upshot of it all is, I'm back at Egerton Hall, ready to sit the exams for Oxford and Cambridge, just before Christmas. I knew all along, of course, that I would be coming back if my results were satisfactory, but it has been so easy, over this long summer holiday, to forget about work and school altogether and turn one's attention to a kind of deliciously lazy sentimental education, which is much pleasanter, that I've let the whole matter of my future slide entirely out of my head.

I'd also got out of the habit of being at home, under the same roof as my father and Marjorie again. My bedroom seemed quite suddenly very small and wrongly decorated, as if some sweet little girl lived there. I'd chosen the wallpaper and the fixtures and fittings myself, so that there was no one I could blame for anything. But had I ever really wanted a dressing-table with white net frills round it? Or a puffy eiderdown covered in burgundy satiny material? As Miss Herbert would have said in our Latin lessons: '*horresco referens*' – I shudder to relate.

'It's lovely to have you back, dear,' Marjorie said to me as we were having a drink before dinner on my very first night at home. I was considered grown-up enough for a small sherry. 'Your father has missed you.'

You haven't, I thought. You've been delighted that I wasn't here.

'And so have I, of course,' she went on. 'You must tell us simply every detail.'

'Oh, it was wonderful!' I gushed. 'We went everywhere: the Louvre, Les Invalides, Notre Dame, even Versailles.'

'But not, alas, to the launderette.' Marjorie shook a finger waggishly at me. 'I've never seen such piles of dirty clothes.'

There was no answer to that. I took a sip of my drink and made an attempt to change the subject.

'I saw one of Alice's aunts while I was there . . . Violette.' Marjorie's brow furrowed.

'Poor Alice!' she said. 'That was a dreadful business. Have you any news of her?'

'Yes, she's very much better, thank you,' I said. Marjorie was hardly listening, still shaking her head as she contemplated that 'dreadful business'. I knew she hadn't given Alice a moment's thought all summer long. I said:

'Do you know someone in Paris called Margot Duboisset?'

Marjorie looked puzzled.

'I don't know a soul in Paris, Bella. You know that.'

'I only asked because . . . well, she looked a little like you. Not as pretty of course, and much older, but there was something.'

'No,' Marjorie shook her head, 'I've never heard of her. How did you meet her?'

'Marion knew her. We went to visit her a couple of times . . . at her flat . . .' (Let it stop, I was thinking, let me change the subject quickly. This lying is harder than I thought. I won't ask about Em.)

'I expect,' Marjorie said, 'you'll be eager for school to start again.'

I was about to make some remark about missing Megan, when I remembered just in time that she was supposed to have been in Paris with me. I made a mental promise to myself never to lie unless I really had to. I said:

'Yes, it'll be fun to see the old place again.'

Marjorie smiled at me and I smiled back, but we had both been speaking in code. She meant: 'I'm longing for you to go, longing for you to get out of this house', and I meant: 'Anything is better than being here with you, even going back to Egerton Hall.'

Just before school started, though, Megan and I went to Arcadia House to spend the weekend with Alice. She is thin now, thinner than she ever was, and her skin is practically transparent, but oh, it was lovely to hear her sounding normal, and being almost exactly like she was before her long . . . I don't know what to call it . . . her long absence from me and Megan. Jean-Luc was there too, and he is completely besotted with Alice, and she flourishes under his gaze like a flower in the sun, so Megan and I feel very happy and also, I think, a little envious.

Arcadia House, which we used to tease Alice by calling the Castle Next Door, was in the process of being restored to its normal state. The gardens, especially, looked terribly neglected and Alice's father seemed to be out in them the whole time we were there, overseeing the care of the roses as his helpers pruned, trimmed, tended and watered all day long.

Megan and I planned to leave Arcadia House on Sunday evening, so Sunday lunch was a farewell celebration.

'I feel like lying down on the nearest bed and sleeping till supper-time,' I said. 'I knew that second helping of apple pie was a mistake. I can hardly breathe, I'm so full.'

'Come for a walk then,' said Alice. 'It'll make you feel better, and in any case I want you and Megan to do me a favour.'

'I can't think of anything I'd rather do less,' I said, 'but this favour sounds mysterious enough to intrigue me. Why can't we do it indoors?'

'You lazy thing,' said Alice. 'You just don't want to move. You can't do this favour inside. It's special.'

So, with me moaning and groaning and Alice and Megan laughing at me, we went into the garden. It was a very warm afternoon. The sun was only visible as a yellow blur behind thin cloud, and the air was heavy. I noticed that on the trees a few of the leaves had begun to turn red and brown. Summer was nearly over. We made our way round the side of the house and over the terraced lawns at the back.

'We're going to the summerhouse,' said Alice. 'We're going to do a – I've forgotten what you call it – one of those ceremonies where you shoo ghosts away from a place.'

'An exorcism,' said Megan. 'Why do we have to do an exorcism here?'

Alice had reached the summerhouse and was opening the door and stepping inside. She turned and looked at Megan and me, standing outside on the grass. She said:

'Because this was where it happened. With Angus. I haven't dared come near here since my party, but I feel . . .' She blushed. 'I feel if you two come in here with me I won't be scared of the place any longer. I'll have some different memories.'

We stepped inside. I sat on a wicker chair and Alice and Megan sat very close to one another on a sort of garden bench.

'Are we supposed to say anything special?' Megan said. 'A prayer?'

'No,' said Alice. 'Just being here is enough. Just talk naturally.'

'Whenever someone tells me to talk naturally,' I said, 'I can't think of a single word to say.'

Alice laughed rather nervously and looked around. She said, rather in the manner of a hostess making conversation:

'Do you still want to go to Oxford, Bella?'

I said:

'I'm not sure any more. Everyone's been persuading me for so long. Megan, you're the worst.'

'It'll be lovely,' said Megan. 'You'll see. Nothing but pleasure every minute of the day.'

'Listen to her,' I said to Alice. 'She always paints these wonderful pictures of us lying around in punts under willow trees with young men of the utmost desirability, or else we're going to balls in flouncy dresses, or acting and singing in all those college productions. She never mentions lectures or tutorials or writing essays for hours on end.'

'Work,' said Megan, 'has never been any trouble to you, Bella. You'll just sail through all of that and hardly notice it.'

I said, 'That's all very nice and fine, but I'll tell you what really persuaded me in the end. It wasn't the teachers or you or my dad. It was Marjorie.'

'Marjorie!' Alice looked puzzled. 'Isn't it rather unlike you to do something Marjorie wants?'

I laughed. 'Well, she says things like: "Think of the fun! Think of the people you'll meet! Oh, it'll be splendid!" but even as she's enthusing away like billy-o, I can hear a thin, greenish sort of tinge of envy in her voice, and that made my mind up for me. The way I look at it is: if Marjorie is going to suffer pangs of one sort or another because I'm at university, then that's a good enough reason for trying to get in.'

'Besides,' said Megan, 'I might be there too. Alice, if only you'd come back as well, we could all be together for another three years.'

Alice shook her head. 'I'm not clever enough. And I hate exams. I hate them much worse than you two do. I shall try and get into Art School, I think, but next year.' She looked down at her hands. 'I have to do what the doctors call "taking it easy" for a bit. I'm going to France to meet Jean-Luc's relations, and then I'll come back and do a secretarial course or something.'

'And you can come and meet us,' said Megan, 'wherever we are and whatever we're doing.'

'Greg,' I said, 'is sulking because I'm going back to school. He thinks that singing his songs for ever to twenty people in a dark cellar should be the height of my ambition.'

'And isn't it?' Megan said. 'Won't you sing with the band again?'

'Of course I will,' I said, 'but only when I can. I've told them that next term is out of the question, at least until the exams are over, but you never know. I might not get into either Oxford or Cambridge and in that case I may very well decide to become a singer. But,' I added, 'there's not a lot of money in it.'

'The band could become amazingly famous,' Alice said.

'And then again,' I said, 'it could remain amazingly obscure!'

We went on talking and talking through the afternoon, until the shadows of the trees lengthened on the grass, and Megan said:

'This bench has become jolly hard, all of a sudden. I think we should go in.'

'Yes,' Alice said and stood up. 'It's getting late, if you want to get back to London tonight.'

Then, suddenly, a silence fell in the summerhouse. Don't they call that an angel passing over? I thought: here we are, all three of us sitting together, talking, and it may be for the very last time. This picture I could see of me and Megan and Alice in the summerhouse was laid over countless other images that came flooding into my mind of us lying about on our beds in the Tower Room, sprawling about in the grass next to the cricket pitches, walking together around the Rim of the Known World, sighing over our homework in the JPR – all of them in the past, gone for ever. I was going to say something, something about my feelings, but I didn't in the end. I felt sad, though. There were Simon and Jean-Luc to think about now, and I had a kind of vision of Alice in the future sitting in this garden with children playing around her. It would never, never be only the three of us ever again. This, I thought, this is the end of my childhood.

On the way up to the house, I asked Alice:

'Did we do it? Did we exorcise all your bad memories?' She smiled and said, 'Maybe. I hope so. I won't know until the next time I go in there. But I hope so. And thank you.'

'There's nothing,' said Megan, 'to thank us for. I wish we could have made it never happen. I wish we could have done more to help you through it.'

Alice shook her head. 'No,' she said, 'don't talk about it any more. It's over now. Finished. Done with. And nothing but nice things to look forward to from now on.'

'Right,' I said. '"Happy ever after" – that'll be our motto. Let us drink a toast to this motto in tea!' Megan and Alice both laughed, but we did it anyway. We went into the kitchen and solemnly raised our teacups and banged them gently together.

'Happy ever after!' we said in unison, and burst out giggling as though we'd made the funniest joke in the world.

Now Alice is in France with Jean-Luc, and Megan and I are back at school. Not in the Tower Room, alas, but in two single rooms next door to one another, which they think is more fitting for such grown-up girls.

Every time I come back to Egerton Hall, as every term begins, I'm amazed at how distant this place is from the real world. I feel like someone who's travelled at the speed of light from one planet to another. The world of boarding-school is so removed from anything else that it's easy to forget what has just happened to you in another place. Perhaps I'm two people: home Bella and school Bella.

Megan has gone to help Matron do Weights and Measures. She volunteered. Miss van der Leyden has retired. That is what we have been told, and I imagine she must have gone back to Belgium. She was ill last spring, and what happened to Alice affected her deeply, so I hope she's better now. Alice is not here to miss her. I never had anything against the old thing, but was never one of her special favourites. Now, both Megan and I are in the very strange position of being the senior girls in the House, and yet having no real authority. Head of House, Second Head, Games Captain: these offices with their attendant obligations of list-making, supervision of people at all sorts of inconvenient times, etc. etc., are taken by girls in the second year Sixth. They've let us keep our Prefects' badges and the privileges that go with them, which is all I care about. We are allowed to go out on Saturday afternoons four times a term at least, and that's something. I can't help feeling we shouldn't be here at all. I said so to Megan this morning.

'I feel,' I said, 'like Gulliver, or something. Too large for this place. All those little first-formers look like ants to me. I feel I've grown up over the summer, Megan, and it's pathetic, after everything that's happened this hols . . . don't you feel like Alice in Wonderland this term? As if everything's very small and you're growing and growing and pushing against the walls, longing to escape?' Megan thought a bit about this before she answered. You could even say 'she considered'. She does a lot of that and I do almost none. Talk first, think later is more my philosophy. Anyway, Megan considered, then said:

'No, actually, I feel I've got smaller. Not physically, but next to the work that has to be done. I mean, up until last term, we always knew exactly what we had to do. This Oxbridge stuff is a bit of an unknown quantity, really. I mean, exams are all very well, but then there are those awful interviews. If you pass the exams, of course. Everyone says it's really the interviews that count, and I shall be tongue-tied, I know I shall.'

'Rubbish,' I said. 'You will impress everyone with the depth of your learning and the maturity of your calm exterior. I, on the other hand (if I pass the exams, as you say), will sizzle and dazzle and bat all available eyelashes etc. I will wear a very short skirt and very high heels.'

Megan giggled. 'Miss Herbert will never let you leave Egerton Hall looking like that! And anyway, it'll all be wasted. They'll all be female dons interviewing you.'

I sighed. 'How sad! I *did* imagine distinguished chaps with greying hair and mortar boards . . . I hoped to bring stirrings of youth and beauty into their crusty old hearts. Never mind! Even for ladies, I see no reason to lower one's standards of dress. You, Megan, are an innocent. I never said anything about leaving Egerton Hall in my outfit. Oh, no!'

'What then? Buck up and tell me. I've got to go and help with Weights and Measures.'

'Poor old you,' I said. 'You have clearly never heard of that quaint, old-fashioned custom: Changing in the Ladies' Room at Victoria Station. Should we go to our interviews together, I will show you how it's done. You, too, Megan, can sizzle and dazzle with a bit of help from me.'

I could hear Megan giggling in the corridor as she disappeared in the direction of Matron's room. Rather her than me. All those skinny kids in school vests and dressing-gowns. There's a craze for quilted nylon at the moment, I've noticed. It's always in ghastly pinks and blues and lemon yellows, and a particularly nasty shade of minty pale green. Ugh! The truth of the matter is I'm fed up to the back teeth with school and all its doings. I feel as if my entire life has been spent at Egerton Hall. I know, I know, every single argument that Megan and all my teachers and my father and everyone else puts to me about the value of education is obviously right and that's why I'm doing it, but I don't see why it has to be hedged in with rules and regulations. I feel ludicrous in my school tunic and that's that. I feel lumpy and the wrong shape for everything. My feet feel as though they belong to someone else, and I get a shock every time I catch a glimpse of them in these terrible, clomping lace-up shoes.

All through school, we've dreamed of food, and now joining the food dreams are the clothes dreams. My nights are filled with images of the red dress I wore in Paris, and I think: was that really me? The same person I am now? I long for wickedly beautiful patent-leather winklepickers with dangerously thin, high heels, skin-tight drainpipe trousers and floating, silky-feeling blouses. I have fantasies of chiffon scarves around my neck, and enormous pendants dangling on the fronts of fluffy jumpers in the rich, dark colours of antique jewels. Then, after all these dreams, I wake up when the bell goes (another horror, another indignity – all of us ordered about all the time as though we were in the army) and just looking at my bra hanging on the back of the chair depresses me. I made the mistake of saying so to Megan. She looked quite astonished.

'It's a bra, Bella. Only a bra. It's designed to stop you from wobbling about all over the place. How can it possibly depress you?'

'I give up,' I answered. 'I do, honestly. If you think all a bra has to do is stop you from wobbling – and I *do* like the elegant way you put that, I must say – then you've got a lot to learn.'

I tried my hardest to look enigmatic and superior so that Megan would beseech me for further enlightenment in the matter of Bras: Their Meaning and Function, but she only shook her head as if to say, 'Poor Bella! All worked up about such trivia . . .' and pointed out to me that if we didn't get a move on, we'd be late for first lesson.

I blame Dorothy. I can't say I've given that much thought to her underwear, but it's quite likely to be armour-plated. How could poor Megan ever discover all the delights of luxurious lingerie with such a person to set her an example? There are occasions (rare, admittedly) when I'm quite grateful to Marjorie for being the kind of woman she is.

I'd never realized how much time we used to spend simply having lessons when we were in the lower forms. Hours and hours on end were taken up, it seems, walking along the corridors from one classroom to another, and listening to teachers doing their bit in turn. It's all quite different now.

The day has become a kind of tundra, a flat, dull expanse only broken up by the odd meal and the odd class. These hours, stretching from breakfast till supper, Megan and I and the other Oxbridge entrants are supposed to fill usefully. When not actually being taught, we are supposed to be in the library reading what everyone and his uncle has said about every single one of our set authors. We are also supposed to read 'more widely' which really means anything even vaguely relevant to our subject.

'It's altogether too much,' I moaned to Megan. 'One can have a surfeit of even the greatest literature. Although I notice that you don't have trouble filling your day.'

'That's because,' Megan said, 'I write poems whenever I feel bored.'

'I can't write poems,' I said.

'Bet you can,' Megan said. 'You've never tried.'

'I sort of feel that if I can't be Rimbaud I'd rather not bother.'

'Then write to Alice,' Megan said.

'There's nothing to write *about*,' I grumbled. 'I'm not doing anything interesting. Alice doesn't want to know about imagery in Leconte de Lisle and Théophile Gautier. Even I don't want to know about it, when you get right down to it.'

'But I've seen you writing,' Megan said. 'You must be writing something.'

'If it's a toss-up,' I answered, 'between my innermost thoughts or an essay on "The Alexandrine is the perfect metre for Classical Tragedy. Discuss," then innermost thoughts win every time. In any case, it's addictive, isn't it?'

'A bit like talking to the perfect listener.' Megan nodded absently. Half her mind was on something else. 'One who never answers back or contradicts you.'

There is nothing for it. I am going to have to translate a chunk of Henry James into French, after first of all (as Megan rather wittily put it) translating the passage into English that normal people can understand.

A letter has come from Alice. Megan and I raced off to the study with it after breakfast. Now I shall have to answer her. Goody goody!

Dear Megan and Bella,
   You are lucky to hear from me at all, because I am having such a wonderful time that I find it hard to tear myself away from what's going on even for a few minutes. But my heart goes out to the two of you, still there at Egerton Hall, working away for still more awful exams, and I think I should try and cheer you up a bit with a letter. It'll give you something to look forward to at breakfast if I start writing to you regularly.
   Jean-Luc's family live in a castle! It's only a little castle, but it's by a river and it's got turrets and spiral staircases all over the place and there are vineyards all around it and the sun is still shining even though it's September.
   He's got a *huge* family. Not as many aunts as I have, but any number of extra little branches of the family tree who keep appearing when you least expect them. *Grand'mère* (as he calls his mother's mother) is a terrifying old bony creature with a pince-nez and black clothes who stares all the time and pinches the tops of my arms and makes 'tsk'ing noises like the witch out of Hansel and Gretel, waiting for me to get plump so that she can eat me! His other granny is fat and jolly, thank goodness, and much given to kissing me and calling me '*petite poupée*'.
   Jean-Luc and I do an awful lot of visiting. I think I'm

being scrutinized by the whole family, to see if I come up to scratch. When we can get away from relations and three-hour-long meals, we go for swims in the river and walks through the countryside. I shan't describe the meals. It'd be cruel to poor old you, still having to endure marge on your toast and rice pudding at least once a week.

I'm so happy, Megan and Bella, that I sometimes feel a bit guilty. I wish you could be here too, though, and I'd really love a letter. It'd be almost like a chat. I'd like to know what's going on at good old Egerton Hall. I miss it sometimes, much more than I miss Arcadia House. I suppose that's not so surprising, since my recent memories of home aren't all that entrancing.

Someone somewhere is preparing an enormous some-thing-or-other for supper. I can smell fresh herbs and wine cooking slowly. Enough! Stop! I can hear you cry, so I shall torment you no further. Back you go to your soggy cabbage and gristly meat . . . Do write soon if poss.

Tons of love,
Alice.

P.S. Can you find out Miss van der Leyden's address? Matron would know, I'm sure. Many thanks.

Chère Princesse Lointaine,

I wish you weren't so 'lointaine', I do honestly. Still, Megan and I are both thrilled to bits that at long last you are living where you belong, i.e. in a castle. I'm writing for both of us, because Megan is in a *total tizzy* and cannot put pen to paper.

Alice, on no account are you to turn the pages to see *why* M. is in this state. That would be cheating.

There is no news. All we ever do is work, work, work.

Nineteenth Century now, all Romantic and Decadent stuff. Baudelaire is *tremendous*, full of sex and drugs and booze and the joys of living life to the full. I'm in love with Rimbaud, as you know, and apart from that, it's not too exciting.

Which brings me to my story. Last Saturday, Megan and I decided that we could bear Egerton Hall not one moment longer, so down we went to the Old Forge for a comforting guzzle. We had the usual. (Let me list it for you, Alice dear, in case the pots-au-feu and the tartes have addled your brain): Welsh rarebits, chips and teacakes. Remember? Doesn't it just make you want to rush back here tomorrow? Anyway, where was I? Yes, imagine M. and me sitting in the gloaming of the Old Forge, quietly tucking in and for once silent, absorbed in our munchings. We're sitting at that table right in the corner, under the sloping bit of the ceiling. Megan's facing the restaurant and I'm opposite her with my back to the door. After a few minutes' worth of chewing, I look up at Megan because she's making a funny noise in her throat, a cross between choking and gasping for breath.

'You've gone completely white, Megan,' I say. (She looked so dreadful that I quite forgot my chips – imagine!) 'Whatever's wrong?' She says nothing, but just sits there staring at the door. Honestly, Alice, it was just like Macbeth seeing Banquo's ghost. She even pointed a trembling finger over my shoulder. So I turn round to look at what she's seeing, and guess what? There's Simon, standing by the door, staring back at Megan in a pretty Macbeth-ish way himself.

Well, I can see at a glance that if Simon keeps standing there, no one can get in or out of the door, so I make a decisive move. Megan, I know, if she's left to her own devices, will just continue sitting in a trance with her fork clutched in her left hand, like Excalibur or something. So I wave and shout:

'Yoo-hoo! Simon! Come over and sit down,' or something equally discreet and elegant. Megan wakes up out of her daze to scold me for being embarrassing, but my shout has the desired effect and soon Simon is sitting with us. He declines Welsh Rarebit and chips and teacake (what devastation Love can wreak!) and orders tea. Megan stops eating altogether, which doesn't worry me. I just finish everything on her plate while they gaze into one another's eyes. Well, gazing has its place, I'd be the first to admit, and far be it from me to be a Preventer of Gazing. Still, I feel a little information wouldn't come amiss, so I start the ball rolling, conversationally. I say:

'I thought you were in America. Megan said you'd got a job.'

Simon says:

'I was never really happy there. As soon as I got there, I was thinking of ways of coming back. I've got a job here now, in a school near London. It's not much, but it's a start. At least I'm getting paid.'

I say:

'That's wonderful! Isn't that wonderful, Megan? Simon's going to be living in London.'

Megan is still silent, still staring at poor Simon as if her eyes could gobble him up and to be fair, he's looking a trifle gobbly, too. Then he says:

'Megan, will you come for a walk with me? Just for a bit? Please.'

Megan still can't bring herself to speak, so I answer for her.

'What a good idea!' I say, noting that the teacakes we

ordered have arrived at the table. 'Go on, Megan. I'll see you back at school. You've got ages. Till six o'clock.'

Megan nods at me, and they walk out of the Old Forge together. I'm so intrigued by what they might do when they get on to the pavement that I stop eating for a full five minutes and crane my head to look out of the window. What can I say, Alice? For the whole time I'm looking at them, they are absolutely *welded* together, starting at the mouth and carrying on to their knees. Welded and entwined. I was thrilled, Alice, I can tell you. I never knew Megan had it in her to stand on a public street *in her Egerton Hall uniform* kissing a man!! In the end, they separated themselves and began to walk away. I ate both teacakes, as a kind of celebration.

Megan arrived back at school at six o'clock, looking like a rosy sleepwalker.

'Where did you go?' I asked.

'For a walk,' Megan said, and then the bell went. I know you think I'd have interrogated her, Alice, asked her what happened, wanted to know details, etc. etc. but I didn't. I was good. You'd have been proud of me. I just felt happy that Megan was happy again, and I was content to leave it at that, only *the best is yet to come*. At about midnight that night, Megan came into my room.

'Are you awake, Bella?' she whispered.

'No, I'm sleeptalking,' I said.

'I'm sorry, only I've got to tell someone . . .'

'Tell,' I said. 'Tell at once.' I was sitting bolt upright by this time as you can imagine.

'It's Simon,' said Megan. 'He's asked me to marry him.' I fell flat on my back and pulled the covers over my face. I had an instant awful vision of Megan leaving the next morning, all dolled up in orange blossom and tulle, and me grinding along here with the exams all on my own. I said:

'What did you tell him?'

'I told him I'd think about it.'

I started laughing then and couldn't stop. Honestly, Alice, can you imagine a more Megan-ish answer??

Anyway, the long and the short of it is: they are Back Together Again, and Megan is Blissfully Happy, and you may or may not be a bridesmaid very soon. Watch this space for more news.

Do you realize I should have been working instead of scribbling all this? If I fail these exams, I shall blame you. All your fault for not being here, Where the Action is.

Megan sends her love and says she will write soon. She has read this letter and shaken her head over it. *Tant pis!*

Loads of love,
Bella

P.S. Write soon.

I am finding it increasingly difficult to concentrate on my work. It's not that the work is uninteresting, but other things keep happening that push it to the side of my attention. I have only to immerse myself in something or another and wham! there's an event. Megan's announcement of Simon's proposal was like that. We have talked of little else since then and Megan veers between wanting to leave school this very minute and fly to Simon's side for ever and ever, and saying things that sound altogether too much like the sensible advice dished out by women's magazines, e.g: 'If he really loves me, then he'll wait for me.'

'That's all very well,' I said, 'but how long can he be

expected to hang around waiting? The whole three years that you're at university? I call that a bit much.'

'Well,' Megan blushed, 'perhaps it is. Maybe I won't get into Oxford or Cambridge. Then I could go to London University, so as to be near him. Maybe I should do that anyway. What do you think?'

'How about Simon looking for a job at Oxford or Cambridge so as to be near you? Do you think he'd consider that? It's funny, isn't it, how we, the women, are always ready to drop our plans at a moment's notice to fit in with men. Do they ever do the same for us?'

'Gosh,' said Megan. 'I hadn't thought of it like that. I could ask him, I suppose. But are you allowed to go up to Oxford and Cambridge if you're married?'

'I've no idea. You needn't marry, of course. He could get a flat and you could be in your college and no one need ever know he's more than your boyfriend . . . though I don't know quite what's supposed to happen to the droves of admirers we were both going to have. I suppose I shall have to cope with them all by myself. Ah, me, a sorry pickle indeed!'

'I feel sometimes,' said Megan, snapping her books shut with an irritation I'd never seen her show before, 'that I'd like to take every single one of my notes and essays and snip them into a million pieces, toss them out of the Tower Room window and let them all drift down over the grass like snowflakes. I'm fed up to the back teeth with all this . . .' She made a gesture that took in the study, the books, and also, it seemed to me, the whole school and her past life. 'I'd like to be someone whose life is straightforward.'

'No, you wouldn't,' I said. 'That'd be too boring for words. All the people with straightforward lives are sitting about longing for complications, for a bit of interest.'

'I know,' said Megan. 'I know. Don't take any notice of me. I expect I'm just tired.'

It's easy to feel tired. We are both working so hard and trying to learn and memorize so much that it's a wonder we don't collapse under the strain. I have these mad fantasies at times, imagining what Rimbaud and Baudelaire and people of that ilk (who were all busy, busy, busy living life to the full, drinking and taking drugs and plunging, as Baudelaire put it, into the depths of the Abyss to find the New) would think of uniformed British schoolgirls writing neat notes about their poetry and considering the meaning of all their soul-shattering experiences. It's quite surreal. And all this cramming is not useless. Not at all. One learns fascinating things, such as this: the poet Gérard de Nerval used to tie a silk ribbon round the neck of his pet lobster and take it for walks along the streets of Paris. I find I can hardly remember the streets of Paris and I was there only weeks ago. The other day, Megan let me read all the letters I wrote her during the holidays, and I found it strange. Did I really feel that strongly about Mark? I realize with a bit of a sinking of the heart that I'm not Dante-and-Beatrice material after all. It's frightfully disappointing. It would have been deeply romantic to come back to school and go into a decline. Matron would have found no cure for such a state. I could have gone and wept at her door, in my own version of the 'Song of Songs':

'Stay me with Syrup of Figs, comfort me with Bovril, for I am sick of Love!' Alas, I think what's wrong with me is I'm too practical. I've managed to banish Mark almost completely from my thoughts. The front of my mind is always full of *now*. I'm not a bit like Megan and Alice who can both somehow manage to focus on their beloveds with a startling tenacity, whether they're there or not. On several occasions, it's true, I've woken up after a dream in which I knew I was on the edge of seeing his face again, but somehow it's always turned away. These dreams are unsettling. I have had to walk along the dim corridors for a bit to calm myself down. Egerton Hall has a special look about it at night. It's what I think of as a hospital look. The passages are lit by dim bulbs under antiseptic white lampshades. The flexes hang from the ceiling at intervals, and from my bedroom to the bathroom at the other end of the corridor, I can count four lights. The glow is pale and bluish and although the doors of all the rooms are closed, I know there are hospital-type beds in each one, with white-painted metal bedheads. It was worse in the Junior House. There we slept in dormitories like open tunnels and there was one light just outside each end. I hated getting up in the night to go to the lavatory, walking past the dark, curtained opening of each cubicle. I used to fix my eyes on the brightness at the end of the tunnel and walk towards it swiftly without turning my head either to left or right. Part of me, the normal, daytime part, knew that it was friends of mine in bed and asleep in every cubicle, but the night-time is a great transformer. I couldn't be sure what had replaced them in their beds with the coming of the dark. I remember this now and think what a silly child I used to be. The night is my favourite time of all now, when the bells have stopped and so have the voices of hordes of noisy girls, and the clever words of the teachers are put away till the morning.

Très chère Alice,
    I think I have been indirectly responsible for one of the most exciting moments the school has seen since Megan and Simon ran away. Last Sunday morning when we all filed into Chapel, who do you think was there, right in the front row of the Gallery in the usual all-black get-up? You'll never guess in a million years so I'll tell you. It was

Greg. Every head was turned to look at him for sixty per cent of the time at least, and you could hear the Juniors twittering and giggling and wondering whose he was, so to speak . . . could he be a Brother? If so, then whose? He'd shaved for the occasion, and his hair had obviously just been washed and flopped over on to his forehead in a way perfectly designed to fill the daydreams of pewfuls (pewsful?) of fourteen-year-olds for months to come. Perhaps I have been taking him for granted, Alice. His eyes are somewhat spectacular, I have to admit. Or is it that being closeted away from all male company has this effect on me, as well as on those silly little girls?

I realized at once, of course, that something very important must have happened to bring Greg down to Egerton Hall. I spent most of the service worrying about what it could be. He was waiting for me outside Chapel when we came out.

'Hello,' he said. 'Bet you're surprised to see me, aren't you?'

'Yes . . . I mean, I'm delighted, but you might have warned me.'

'It was spur of the moment. I had the use of a car. Can I take you out of this place?'

'We'd have to go and find Miss Herbert.'

'Do I have to come? Can't I wait by the car?'

'No, I think she needs to see you. Make sure you're respectable.'

'Oh, Lord!' Greg groaned. 'If I'd known I'd have to meet a teacher, I'd have stayed in London.'

I dragged him off to Miss Herbert's study. She was chatting to some parents, so we waited by the polished table in the Front Hall. When Miss Herbert finally emerged, Greg was showing an enormous interest in the grandfather clock by the stairs. Well, I introduced them and he hummed and ha'ed and shuffled his feet, but he did manage a reasonable facsimile of a smile at one point and honestly, Alice, I could see Miss Herbert thaw out before my very eyes. She put her hand up to her bun and patted it in a way that was almost flirtatious. She smiled back at him. I think, though I'm not quite sure, that she referred to us as 'you young people', sounding positively benevolent.

'She's rather nice,' said Greg as we disappeared down the drive at high speed in a dangerous-looking little red thing he swore was a car, and it came to me with a bit of a shock that she, too, must have been young once. Do you remember how we used to invent a love-life for her, when we were in about the Upper Third? Anyway, I digress. Where do you think we went? Three guesses. Right first time: the Old Forge.

I said: 'To what do I owe the pleasure of a visit from you?'

'I've got some news,' Greg answered, 'so I thought I'd come and tell you and get out of London for the day at the same time.'

'First things first,' I said, and smiled over his head at the waitress. 'I heartily recommend the Welsh Rarebit. The teacakes are good, too. Also the chips. They do very good chips.'

'But it's only half past eleven,' said Greg. 'On normal days I wouldn't even be getting up yet.'

'You are a dissolute jazz musician,' I said, 'but I am a healthy English schoolgirl. It's hours and hours since breakfast. If you prefer, I can refer to this as an early lunch.'

He sighed. We ordered Welsh Rarebit and chips for me, and a cup of coffee for him.

'Right,' I said. 'Tell me all the news.'

'Well,' said Greg, 'the thing is we've been asked to do the cabaret at a twenty-first birthday party in December. This friend of Roddy Maxton's heard us at his party and is willing to pay us bundles of money on condition that you're with us. You will do it, Bella, won't you? He's taken quite a shine to you, this Ackworth chap.'

'Gosh,' I said, shovelling in the chips, 'that sounds great. Is it after the twelfth or will I have to climb in and out of school like I did for the Valentine's Day thing?'

'It's the fourteenth, so that's okay,' Greg said, 'only there is one tiny drawback.'

'Go on, tell me. I shan't collapse.'

Greg sighed. 'It turns out that the Ackworth family are patients of your dad's. I'm afraid that he's invited to the party and so is Marjorie.'

'I've changed my mind,' I said. 'I think I will collapse after all.' I grinned. 'No, I don't really mean it. I haven't any objections to singing in front of Marjorie. In fact, I'd quite enjoy it, if you want to know the truth. And there'll be crowds of people there, so we won't have to speak to them or sit with them or anything. Where's it being held, this do?'

'At a nightclub in Pimlico called The Glass Menagerie.'

'It sounds frightfully exclusive. That's because I've never heard of it.'

'I've never been there either,' said Greg, 'and we aren't going to get a chance to rehearse there until the morning of the party, but I gather from Phil that it's weird. A weird place.'

'Whatever do you mean?' I asked.

'I'm just repeating what Phil said. He said the decor was surrealistic and when I asked him what he meant, he shook his head and said, "Weird, man, really weird." And Rilly says . . .' Greg blushed and I looked at him, hard.

'Have you been seeing the Pink Marshmallow of London Town while I've been slaving away over a hot textbook?'

'No, no,' Greg stammered. He was still blushing. 'She and Roddy just came round one night for a drink. Honestly, that's all it was.'

'It's okay. Only don't go on protesting too much or I shall decide not to believe you.'

'No, please, Bella. Please believe me . . .' he said.

'All right,' I said. 'I'll believe you if you order me a toasted teacake.'

After the teacake, Greg drove me back to school, and we managed a very loving smooch in the front seat of the car before I got out. I wonder if anyone managed to see us. They must certainly have heard the car coming up the drive, gone to the windows to have a look, and then counted the minutes until I got out and wondered feverishly exactly what was going on in there! Tee, hee!

It's taken me ages to write all this. Please make sure you write back.

Love,

Bella

The examinations are over.

It came to me in a rush right in the middle of my Spanish Translation paper that I had no desire whatsoever to spend the next three years reading texts in foreign languages, and putting down my thoughts about them in yet another long series of three-hour examinations. This revelation terrified me, and I continued with the Spanish Translation paper and all my other papers without saying a word to anyone, not even to Megan. She, I know, is dreaming of extending our time in school together for another three years. How can I tell her that the thought appals me? I have decided to say nothing and hope for the best. Most people, it has to be said, don't even get as far as an interview. I shall have to keep my fingers crossed. Now that the papers are over, I find it difficult to know how well or badly I've done. I suppose if I were really serious, I would have withdrawn from the whole examination, or sat at my desk and written nothing, but I couldn't do that to my teachers, who would have been so upset. As it is, if I don't make it to the interviews, they can mutter darkly about prevailing standards, bias among the markers, etc. etc. I haven't given any thought at all to what I could do instead of going to university. Personally, I'd be quite happy to go on singing with the band and leading a Bohemian existence in London, however uncomfortable such a life is sometimes, but what (if I don't become famous, which is more than likely) would I live on? It would be good to discuss this with someone, but Alice isn't due back here till the end of the month, and Megan . . . I daren't tell Megan any of this.

'Well,' said Miss Herbert, 'this has all come to pass in a very satisfactory manner.'

Megan and I, sitting in front of her desk on the two upright chairs reserved for parents being lightly grilled about their offspring, nodded politely.

'It is, perhaps, regrettable that you will be travelling to different destinations, but we must not be churlish. One interview each at Oxford and Cambridge is very creditable. Very creditable indeed. You may travel as far as London together on Monday afternoon and spend Monday night . . .?'

'At my parents' house . . .' I put in.

'Precisely. At the house of Dr and Mrs Lavanne and the next morning you can set off to your respective London termini.'

'Could we possibly leave on Monday morning?' I asked. 'I'd love to get my hair done in the afternoon.'

Miss Herbert's expression and tone did not alter, but a twinkle of amusement crossed her face.

'Naturally, I cannot imagine a place at one of our great universities being casually handed out to someone who appears for her interview . . . how shall I put it? . . . inadequately coiffed.' She stood up, thus telling us that our little interview was over.

Outside Miss Herbert's door, Megan said:

'Are you really going to have your hair done?'

'Certainly,' I said, 'what did you think I'd be doing?' From Megan's blush, I knew at once.

'You thought I'd rush straight round to Greg's for a spot of slap and tickle, didn't you?'

'Well . . .'

'Just because you're spending Monday night chez Simon . . .'

'Ssh . . .'

'It's all right, her door's closed. Anyway, there'll be no chummy changing into clothes in station loos together, will there? I call it a bit of a swizz. I don't know that I want to go to Cambridge, especially not without you.'

'Oh, Bella, not that again! Why not?'

'There's so much else I'd rather be doing than studying things and learning stuff and putting it all pointlessly down on paper.'

'You'll feel better,' said Megan, 'once you see the place. I'm sure you'll love it.'

'No, you're not,' I said. 'The only thing you're sure of is that *you'll* love it.' That's a different thing altogether.'

'Oh, for heaven's sake,' said Megan. 'They may not offer a place to either of us. Let's not quarrel about it.'

'Let's not,' I agreed. 'Let's talk about Armand's instead. Are you going to come with me?'

'No, I think there's very little he can do to my hair.'

'He could trim it,' I suggested.

'I think I'd be bald if he did,' Megan laughed.

'But you don't mind if I do, do you?'

'Certainly not,' she said. 'I shall be otherwise occupied.'

'I'll bet you will be.' I laughed and we went upstairs together to sort out garments with which to bewitch those who would be interviewing us.

Armand's salon was as delicious as ever. This, I thought, must be a little what Paradise is like. Whatever is worrying you, whatever troubles you may have in this chilly, grey November world outside, you simply hang up along with your outdoor coat in the cupboard by the entrance. Then you put on the rose-pink robe and at once peace and contentment settle around you.

'Mam'selle Bella! It is such a long time!' Armand was gratifyingly pleased to see me. 'No one has seen you. Madame Lavanne, she has stopped speaking of you almost completely. You 'ave been, how do they say? Living it up?'

I laughed. 'Whatever gave you that idea? I've been stuck at school with my head in a book for nearly three months.'

'Aah, le midnight oil! *Je comprends*. It is for that that you have the eyeshadows under the eyes.'

'Well, that's all over now. I doubt very much if I shall study anything more taxing than the *Tatler* ever again.'

Monsieur Armand said: 'And here he is, the new *Tatler*,

just for you. You will sit and study him while I comb out Madame La Contesse, then I will focus on you all my attention.'

The *Tatler* was full of girls who looked like Rilly Maxton popping out of strapless ballgowns and showing overtoothy grins to the cameras. None of the men looked at all desirable. I was so bored by the whole magazine that I nearly missed it. At first, I glanced at the page (a party in a castle in Scotland) and turned over, but some whisper, some half-glimpsed something made me turn back. I looked at each picture more closely and there it was, right in front of my eyes, at the very top of the right-hand page, on the right-hand side. At first it seemed to be like all the others: a photograph of some revellers in evening dress, but one of the faces was the face I had almost (but not quite) forgotten about, the face I'd first seen in the Club Sortilège in August. I felt cold. My heart started beating very quickly. The print under the photograph swam and danced before my eyes. Left to right, the Hon. this and that, Lord so-and-so, Viscount Thingummy, and then, in very clear black letters: 'Mr Mark Eschen, of Boston, U.S.A.' I stood up and walked over to where Armand was combing out the Countess or whatever she was. I said:

'Armand . . . Armand, please, please can I cut out this photo? Please. It's got someone in it that . . . that I saw once.'

Armand smiled at the Countess in the mirror and murmured something in her ear. Then he picked up his scissors.

'Which photo, *ma petite*? This one? *Voilà*. I cut for you.' Snip, snip went his scissors then he handed me the tiny scrap of paper and pointed straight at Mark.

'*Celui-là, n'est-ce pas?*' he said.

'However did you know?' I was amazed.

'About what you will love,' he said, 'I know a great deal.

This one, *par exemple*, is not your beloved.' He indicated a foxy-looking chap with a bristly moustache.

'Quite right, Armand, you're very clever.'

Later on, when he was combing out my hair, he said:

'So tell me the story. Where did you meet this so handsome young person?'

'I've only met him once. In Paris. He came to the club where I was singing. That's all.'

'But it is so romantic! If he saw you, this young man, if he spoke to you, then he loves you . . . *C'est très simple.*'

It was only when I passed a newsagent's on my way to Sloane Square Underground that I realized I could have bought my own copy of the magazine. I'd been too busy saying to myself, over and over again: he's not in America, he's here. He could be on the same tube; he could appear at any moment! Of course I knew he wouldn't, but it made me feel better to know that at the very least he was on the same side of the Atlantic as I was. I imagined Armand nodding his head knowingly. Lovely Armand! He was very kind to me, but what a lot of nonsense he talked from time to time!

Dearest Alice,

Will this letter reach you, I wonder, before you leave France and come back here to us? I don't suppose it matters, as I can easily tell you everything all over again.

Megan and I are back from our interviews, and we feel more out of place than ever. We are literally just hanging about the school killing time until the dreaded telegrams come or don't come. They send you one if you've got in, and if you haven't you just have to wait until the time for getting them has run out and then call it a day. It's not so bad for me, as I've decided . . . well, I'll tell you everything.

Before I start on my story, you should know that Megan has fallen in love with Oxford, and came back all starry-eyed and ready to throw herself off the nearest cliff if she doesn't get in, so keep your fingers crossed. She has decided that she and Simon will become engaged, and he has undertaken to wait for her until she takes her degree. It must be Love! Meanwhile, he will look for jobs in or around Oxford. They will announce their engagement at the party I've already told you about, the one given by Rilly Maxton's Rich Friend, in that club called The Glass Menagerie. It goes without saying that you are invited. December the fourteenth (my goodness, that's only ten days away . . .) at eight-ish. I'll give you the address nearer the time, but I know it's in Pimlico, just off Lupus Street somewhere.

Back to my interview. I have to say that I most likely didn't see Cambridge at its best. The weather was dank and misty and cold and the college was miles out of town, but still, I looked around the place and came to the conclusion that Seats of Learning are not my cup of tea. Everyone was very kind at the college, which is a red-brick, ivy-clad sort of building, but it's so exactly like school inside that I was quite downcast. As soon as I sat down to supper in what looked like a larger version of the Brontë House dining-room, I knew I couldn't possibly spend the next three years of my life in such a place. By that time I'd already had chats with two scholarly ladies, who had been most kind. I can hardly remember anything of what I said. I was just aware of my heart sinking further and further into my boots. There was to be one more interview after supper, then a night in one of the rooms and then back to London on a train in the morning. Actually, I was quite looking forward to this after-supper interview because it was with Madame Séverine Drouet, the person who wrote that book on Baudelaire . . . do you remember? I was quite excited at the thought of meeting a real live writer, and she was wonderful. Very chatty and friendly and Parisian. I found myself telling her all about my time in Paris, the singing, everything. She listened. She made us coffee (after being extremely rude about the college coffee), she told me about her early days as a student in the Sorbonne, and just as I was on the point of saying good-night and leaving, she looked me straight in the eye and said:

'You have no desire whatsoever to come to Cambridge. Am I right?'

I couldn't think what to answer, Alice. Honestly, I was so embarrassed. But don't you think it was clever of her to know? I couldn't lie. I said:

'No. No, I haven't. But I'm ashamed to tell anyone.' She stood up and I stood up and she walked with me to the door. Then she kissed me on both cheeks.

'*Adieu, ma petite,*' she said. 'Everything will turn out for the best. You will see. I am not at all worried about you.'

All night I lay awake, wondering what she meant. I've come to the conclusion that I won't be offered a place at all and that she will somehow have seen to it. Or maybe she just meant that I wasn't up to the standard anyway . . . it doesn't matter. Either way, I shall have to think of something else to do. You are very lucky to have your Art. Maybe I'll come to secretarial college with you after Christmas while I think what to do.

See you very soon,
Tons of love,
Bella

My letter never reached Alice. I forgot to post it when I got back to school, and on the Sunday after Megan and I returned from our interviews, Alice herself came down to Egerton Hall to take us out for the day. Her appearance in the Visitors' Gallery caused a sensation. All the flocks of juniors who had been devoted to her and had thought her lost for ever couldn't stop whispering and pointing. The Staff tried frowning at them, to quell them a little, but you could see they were half-hearted about it. Alice looked so lovely in a plain blue dress with a black headband holding her hair back from her face that even the Chaplain, I thought, found it difficult to pay attention to the service. After Chapel, we had trouble getting away for our lunch at the Old Forge. Walking through School Corridor was like a Royal Progress. Alice stopped and talked to everyone and smiled and smiled and said yes, she was very much better now, thank you, and Megan and I walked behind her like ladies-in-waiting, fending off those who seemed simply to want to touch her.

It was a huge relief to be out of school and sitting round our usual table in the delicious semi-darkness of the Old Forge. I said:

'Don't anyone dare to say: "It's just like old times." I'll kill them.'

Alice smiled. 'But you've said it!'

'So I have,' I answered. 'So now we've got that over with, thank goodness.'

'It was very strange,' Alice said, 'being back at Egerton Hall. It seems like such ages since I was there.'

'It's us you should feel sorry for,' I said. 'We're like Souls in Limbo now. Neither really at school, nor properly out of it. No more lessons. No more Prep. We just float about, like wraiths, don't we, Megan?'

Megan nodded. 'It's ghastly. We go round and round the

Rim of the Known World on these endless walks, and then we come in and supervise something or other: sit with forms while Staff get on with writing reports – that sort of thing. It's awful. And of course, we wait. Next week we'll know if we've got in.'

'You'll get in,' I said to Megan, 'and I shan't.'

'You don't know that,' Megan said. 'You don't know at all.'

I said nothing and settled in to eating my Welsh Rarebit. Then Megan said:

'You should have seen her, Alice, when she got back from Cambridge. She was like a Fury. Her hair was practically standing on end, she was so cross.'

'What about? What happened? Do tell,' Alice said. I noticed she had hardly touched her food.

'Eat up like a good girl,' I said, 'and I'll tell you.' Alice obediently speared a chip and began nibbling it.

'It was Greg,' I said. 'It all happened while I was having a milkshake, and I could cheerfully have chucked it into his lap, I can tell you.'

'What's he done?' Alice asked. She had finished Chip One and was just about to embark on Chip Two.

'He came to meet me at Liverpool Street and he was supposed to spend a pleasant hour in my company . . . please bear in mind that I am the Light of his Life and his Muse and Constant Inspiration . . . before putting me on to the train at Victoria. So we went into a Wimpy Bar and I ordered my usual treat – one of those chocolate milkshakes that's so thick it can hardly make its way through the straw – and we settled down to discuss arrangements for this twenty-first birthday party on December the fourteenth, and things like whether there would be time for rehearsals, etc. etc. Now I'd noticed, right from the second I saw him at the barrier at Liverpool Street, that all was not well. He kept not looking at me. He held my hand a bit on the tube, but as if he didn't quite want to, if you know what I mean. As if it embarrassed him. Then at the Wimpy Bar, he kept fidgeting and squeezing the plastic tomato on the table. He was making me feel nervous and angry, so I said:

'"Tell me what's on your mind, Greg. You haven't once looked me straight in the eye."

'He looked at me then and looked away at once. He muttered something I didn't hear. I said:

'"Say that again. I didn't hear it."

'He said, "I asked you whether you loved me. That's all."

'Well, I just sat there, quietly turning the colour of the plastic tomato Greg was still prodding in a desultory fashion. I laughed weakly and said:

'"That's a bit of an unexpected question in the middle of a chocolate milkshake."

'"Nevertheless," he said.

'"Nevertheless what?"

'"I want to know the answer," he said.

'Now I was the one to do a bit of looking away. I fiddled with my straw. I sucked on it a bit and managed to persuade a trickle of chocolate into my mouth. I knew I had to tell the truth. I knew I had to be honest even at the risk of hurting Greg's feelings. So I said:

'"No, I don't love you. Not properly love in the way you mean." Then I went gabbling on, trying to soften the blow. "But I'm frightfully fond of you, and I do think you're terrifically good-looking and I love singing your songs." I ended rather lamely, really, by saying, "I like you absolutely masses and masses."

'"But you wouldn't call it love?"

'"No," I said. "I wouldn't call it love. Why ever do you want to know so badly?"

'"Because there is someone. Someone who truly does love me."

'I felt relieved and mildly irritated at the same time. If Greg transferred his affections elsewhere, I would be free . . . free to dream about the face in the *Tatler* photo hidden deep in my purse. Big deal, I thought. I said:

'"Is it anyone I know?"

'"It's Rilly Maxton."

'"You told me she and Roddy had just come round for a drink . . ."

'"That was weeks ago. Things have . . . developed since then."

'"Really?" I said. "I suppose they must have."

'It wasn't the most brilliant thing to say, but I suddenly felt furious and jealous and even more livid with myself because I knew I had no right whatsoever to be jealous. It was just the thought of him kissing that pig-like face. I stood up with as much dignity as I could muster and said something like:

'"I hope you'll be very happy, but I've got to go and get my train now." We left the Wimpy Bar. Greg was much happier after his confession, but I was seething. Just before I got on to the train, I couldn't resist torturing him a bit. I said:

'"Maybe you'd like Rilly to sing at the party instead of me. How would that be?"

'He looked so stricken, turned so white that I instantly took pity on him.

'"Don't be ridiculous, Greg," I said. "Of course I'll do it. For old times' sake, etcetera."

'I got on the train and began to feel miserable, cross and sorry for myself. What was to become of me? I didn't want to go to Cambridge and now I didn't particularly want to live with the band in the house at World's End, and I certainly didn't want to stay at home with Marjorie and her comments and suggestions for ever.'

My narrative must have enthralled Alice. She had finished almost all her food without even noticing what she'd done. Megan said:

'She arrived back at school white-faced and tight-lipped and when I asked her what was wrong, she burst into tears and we were up half the night discussing Life and What Beasts Men Were, etcetera, etcetera. It was just like the good old days.'

Alice said, 'But if you honestly don't love him, Bella, you shouldn't really care.'

'I don't "really care", as you put it. I just feel peeved, and piqued and put out. It's not so much that I want him as that I resent Silly Rilly having him. I mean, I keep thinking: what can she give him that I can't? That's what I want to know.'

'Love,' said Megan, and Alice nodded her agreement.

'What about glamour, excitement, passion, uncertainty, danger? Not to mention Divine Beauty and Unquenchable Talent?'

Alice and Megan shook their heads.

'Not a patch on Love,' said Megan. 'If she really loves him, that's it. She'll get him.'

'She's welcome to him,' I said. 'They will have the most frightfully pink children, if they ever get married. I vote we order our teacakes and talk of happier things.'

I had half-expected the last days at Egerton Hall, the very end of my school career, to be marked by some excitement, but everything happened much as it had always happened in the past.

I found the whole thing a bit of an anti-climax. There was

a flurry of drama when Megan was told of her Oxford place – the Head even declared that there would be a half-holiday next term to celebrate – and murmurings of sympathy and understanding from all the staff who had taught me, who seemed personally wounded by my failure to gain entry to a Cambridge college.

My face, those last few nights at school, was quite stiff from smiling brave and cheerful smiles all day long.

'Thank goodness,' I said to Megan, 'for such things as the Carol Concert to take people's minds off us for a bit.'

'I'm feeling quite strange,' she said, 'leaving this place. You must remember, I've lived here since I was eleven, during the holidays, too. I'm dreading saying goodbye to Dorothy. I shall tell her the truth. She surely can't mind about me living with Simon now, can she? Not if we're actually announcing our engagement?'

'You'd be surprised,' I said. 'I expect she'll always mind, in some part of her. But I shouldn't think she'd dare say anything, not now that you've got into Oxford. She'll just do some inward festering, I expect, much like Marjorie, who will suddenly be faced with the prospect of me in her house again. You should think yourself lucky you've got Simon to go to. Oh, I could kick that Rilly Maxton for ruining the World's End house for me! I really loved it there.'

'Couldn't you stay there anyway?' Megan asked. 'There's tons of space. You need hardly ever see Greg, surely?'

'No, but I couldn't bear to cross the threshold knowing The Pink One is ensconced on my chaise-longue, most probably. No, I shall stick it out with Marjorie until something more interesting presents itself.'

The last morning came, and then the last night. My trunk was full of uniform for the last time. I lay in the dark in my narrow school bed looking at it and thinking: I wish I could heave it out of the train window and into the river on the way in to London. That was the traditional thing to do with a school hat and tie, and mine, I had promised myself, would be first out of the window.

'This time tomorrow,' I muttered to myself,
'where shall I be?
out of the gates
of misery . . .'

I said all the verses I could remember. The last one before I fell asleep was:

'No more beetles
in my bath,
trying hard
to make me laugh.'

'But what,' said Marjorie, taking a delicate spoonful of apple crumble and holding it for a moment in front of her face, 'do you propose to do with your life?'

I waited till I could see her elegantly chewing before I answered.

'I'm not going to do anything till the New Year,' I said. 'I've got the party in a couple of days, and then I'm going to float about and think. Perhaps I'll apply to go to drama school. I'd like that, or I could do a secretarial course, like Alice. Or perhaps a Famous Producer will hear me at this party and make me rich and famous.'

Marjorie turned a little pale.

My father said:

'You don't want to badger the poor girl, my dear. She's had a lot of strain, what with the exams and the disappointment over Cambridge. It'll be a pleasure to have her at home again, as far as I'm concerned. You take all the time you like deciding what to do. We've seen little enough of you, these past few months.'

Marjorie was having some difficulty, I could see, in finishing her apple crumble. It appeared to have glued her teeth together. In the end, though, she did manage some semblance of a smile and said:

'Of course, Bella, you must stay just as long as you like. It'll be quite like the old days!'

'Yes,' I said, 'yes, it will.'

I was thinking: that's what I'm afraid of, and already casting about in my mind for some way of escaping. I had only been here one day, and already the walls were closing in. My apple crumble kept sticking to the roof of my mouth, and nearly choking me. I had to keep taking sips of water in order to get it down at all. Home sweet bloody home, I thought. Let me out.

Marjorie, who was obviously as delighted as I was at the prospect of having me permanently in residence, made a valiant effort to steer the conversation towards pleasanter things.

'Rosemary Ackworth tells me that your friends . . . the musicians . . . are providing the cabaret at Graham's twenty-first birthday party. Now at last we shall hear you sing.' She smiled, as though uncertain whether this was going to be a pleasure or not. 'And Rosemary has asked me to give a dinner party before the dance. Could you possibly come to that, or will you be with your friends?'

I thought of Pete's house, of the band preparing for the party, of Rilly Maxton quite possibly spread all over my chaise-longue.

'Could Megan and Simon come too?' I asked. 'And Alice? Then we could all go on to this nightclub together . . . The Glass Menagerie or whatever it's called.'

'What a frightfully good idea!' said my father. 'I shall feel as though I've come down to Egerton Hall to take you girls out for a slap-up lunch at the Royal George. It'll be quite like old times.'

'Yes,' I said. 'And thank you both. I'll let the others know.' It wouldn't be like old times at all, not one little bit, but whatever happened, at least Megan and Alice and I would be able to face it together.

There was never any question about what I would be wearing to sing at the Ackworths' party. It had to be Madame's red dress – to remind me of Paris, to remind Greg of me and what I had been to him, to remind me of possibilities in my life whose existence I had practically forgotten, and above all to say: there's one in the eye for you, respectable upper-middle-class London, with your princess-line taffetas and your boring old pastel colours!

I'd taken out the dress, and hung it on the back of the door. It could have done with a spot of dry-cleaning, I suppose, but I'd left it too late. I'd ironed all the flounces as best I could, and that would have to do.

As I got ready that evening, I remembered what fun it had been, preparing for Alice's party, only six months ago. Now I couldn't summon up any pleasurable feelings at all.

'In fact,' I said, grimacing at my reflection in the dressing-table mirror, 'you will be smiling though your heart is aching, even though it's breaking, etcetera, etcetera.' I struck a silly pose to cheer myself up. 'The show must go on! On with the motley! Calloo, callay!' I said, and began to decorate my eyes with black lines which would not have disgraced Cleopatra herself. Then Marjorie half-knocked at the door and came in without being asked.

'Bella darling,' she said, 'I was just wondering what you

were going to wear. I can't decide, so I've come to make sure we don't both pick the same colour, or something awful.'

I pointed to the back of the door. Marjorie stared at the dress for a full thirty seconds. Then she turned round to face me.

'But Bella,' she said, 'you can't possibly wear that.'

'Why not?' (Oh, my hand was very steady with the eyeliner brush! I could feel the distant rumbling of a row coming nearer and nearer.)

'Well, for one thing it's filthy.'

'No one'll notice.'

'Of course they'll notice. Have you really learned nothing from me in all these years, nothing about style or fashion, not to mention personal hygiene?'

'There's nothing wrong with my personal hygiene,' I said, 'and as for style, I like that dress. That *is* my style.'

'But it's tarty, Bella. You'll look cheap and tawdry.'

I turned round on my stool and gave her my full attention. I could have avoided what happened next. I could have said something conciliatory and calming, but I didn't want to. The urge to let out all the feelings I'd been bottling up over years was overwhelming, and I felt a thrill of excitement as I opened my mouth, like the sickening lurch of pleasure and terror at the start of a roller-coaster ride. I said, very slowly:

'No, Marjorie, you're wrong. I've worn that dress many times before, and I look terrific. Vibrant, alive, sexy, dangerous, sparkling, beautiful and above all YOUNG. It shows off my white skin with not one wrinkle in it, my breasts that don't yet need the assistance of an architect-designed bra. It flatters my 24-inch – yes, 24-inch – waist, and my black curling tresses. And you can't bear it, Marjorie, because you're not young any more. That's true now, but it hasn't always been. You were young once, too, and more beautiful than I was, and even then you weren't happy. You couldn't face the distant possibility of growing old. You've done everything in your power to hurt me, and I don't care what you say now . . . I don't believe you.'

'How dare you!' Marjorie hissed as I was drawing breath. 'I've been like a mother to you all these years . . .'

'Rubbish,' I shouted, losing all control. 'You have *not* been a mother to me. Nothing like a mother. That's just . . . just *bullshit!*'

Marjorie stiffened and turned to ice.

'It's no more,' she said, 'than what I expect from you . . . a vulgar word like that. Mixing with the kind of people you mix with . . . tatty musicians . . .'

'Get out!' I screamed. 'Get out and leave me alone!'

'It may have slipped your mind,' she answered, 'that I have a dinner party starting in two hours' time. For your father's sake, I would ask you to control yourself and act in a respectable manner.' She smiled at me frostily. 'We have managed this charade very well for many years, Bella. Let us try and bring it off just once more, shall we?'

'You admit it,' I said, exhausted by my outburst. 'You admit it was a charade.'

Marjorie said only: 'I hope you'll be all right at the dinner party. All this shouting will probably have given you a headache.'

'I shall take an aspirin,' I said stiffly.

'In the bathroom cupboard,' Marjorie said, and left the room.

I *did* find some pills in the bathroom cupboard, and took two, even though the packet looked unfamiliar. Then I caught sight of myself in the mirror over the sink. I suppose I must have had tears in my eyes, because the reflection I saw in the glass was fractured, as though my face had been broken up into tiny, glittering pieces.

Whatever they were, the pills must have worked. Everything looked very small and distant to me, as though the dinner party were happening at the other end of a telescope. Megan and Simon and Alice were sitting far away from me. I don't know what I said to my neighbours at the table. I can't remember any of the food. There was not a sign of it on my skin, but I felt as though I'd been repeatedly beaten, as though my whole body were nothing but one enormous bruise.

'You must try some of this, darling,' Marjorie said. 'It's very strong, of course, but absolutely scrumptious.' She handed me a glass full of golden liquid. I took a small sip, and my mouth was filled with the fragrance and taste of apples.

'What is it?' I asked.

'Calvados,' said Marjorie, 'from Normandy. It's a liqueur made from apples.'

I took another sip, but it went down the wrong way, and I began to cough and splutter. From a great distance, I could hear Alice saying:

'Look, Megan! Bella's choking . . . oh Megan, what shall we do?' and because I felt so dizzy I didn't know whether she really did say it, or whether I was remembering the scene that Sunday evening at Egerton Hall, when I'd had a piece of apple stuck in my throat.

'I'm fine,' I whispered after a moment. 'I'll be all right now. Really.'

The band were waiting for me at the Glass Menagerie. It was an extraordinary place.

The tables were black and made of plastic shaped into hands on top of arms that grew out of the floor. The walls were white and hung with huge, disembodied blue eyes and pairs of dark crimson lips.

'Let me explain,' said Phil, who seemed well up in Surrealism, or whatever this was. 'We are in a zoo. A menagerie. We are the animals. Those,' he pointed to the eyes and lips, 'represent the world looking at us, and that,' he nodded to a cage made of glass and thin gold wire which was hanging from the ceiling above the heads of the crowd, 'is a menagerie within a menagerie. That's usually occupied by a dancer, but tonight as a special treat, you are going to be the main attraction.' He beamed. 'We reckon it'll knock them all sideways, you singing your songs from that cage.'

'Well, roll up, roll bloody well up! All the fun of the fair! Bella Lavanne as part of a circus!' I shook my head in disbelief, but it still felt as though it were full of cotton wool. And I didn't care. I didn't care about anything. If they wanted songs sung from a glass cage, well, that was fine with me. I wanted the evening to be over. The taped music was so loud you couldn't hear yourself think, and more and more people were arriving all the time. Squeals of idiotic laughter cut through the noise here and there, and the temperature was rising.

'Do let's find a table, darling,' I heard Marjorie say to my father. 'I should never have worn these new shoes. Every step I take is absolute hell. I don't know how I'm going to stagger through the rest of the evening . . .'

My father chuckled. 'I shan't say, I told you so,' he laughed, 'but I did, didn't I?'

'Oh, really,' Marjorie snorted, 'I don't know how you can be so heartless. I feel as if these shoes have been soldered to my feet with red-hot irons, and that's all you can say!'

A waitress came round with drinks. I turned to Megan and Simon, who were standing beside me.

'Bring your champagne,' I shouted over the din, 'and you, Alice. Come upstairs for a moment. Come outside.'

'We'll freeze to death,' Megan shouted back.

'Only for a minute,' I yelled. 'We have to do this properly. Don't let's lose sight of the fact that we are celebrating your engagement.'

We pushed and struggled through the crowds. When we got outside, the air was inky-blue and icy. The silence sparkled in our ears. We breathed the night in. I caught sight of a white cat disappearing round a corner and I shivered. Don't be silly, I said to myself. London is full of cats. Why shouldn't some of them be white?

'Ladies and gentleman,' I said, 'I give you a toast: Megan and Simon.'

They all drank, and I drank too, and then we solemnly hugged one another.

'Ladies and gentleman,' said Megan, 'I give you another toast: Alice and Jean-Luc, an absent friend.'

'Alice and Jean-Luc!' we cried and Alice's eyes began to glitter suspiciously. Simon raised his glass, and looked at me.

'I'd like to propose a toast to all three of you: the Egerton Hall girls – Megan, Alice and Bella.'

I thought that was sweet of Simon. It made it less obvious that there was no one whose name could be said in the same breath as mine.

'Can we go back in now?' asked Alice. 'I'm so cold.' We laughed, and made our way downstairs.

'It looks,' Alice shouted from halfway down the stairs, 'like one of those pictures of Hell by Hieronymus Bosch.'

'Yes,' I answered, 'only the music's louder.' I noticed Rilly

Maxton dancing with Greg. A blissful smile played over her porky features.

'I'm not in the least jealous,' I said to Alice, 'but how *could he?*'

'She's not bad,' Alice said. 'Be fair. And she loves him. She's . . . buxom, that's all.'

'That's quite enough, I should have thought. Oh, well,' I sighed, 'I suppose I'd better go and get ready for my big moment. Harry's waving at me.'

I walked towards the dance floor. The glass cage had been lowered, ready for me to step into it.

'What about a microphone?' I said, and Pete answered:

'There are mikes concealed in the corners, here and here. You'll be fine.'

I walked into the cage and the doors closed behind me. Then the whole thing was slowly lifted into the air. Looking down, I could see the seven members of the band, much smaller suddenly, and, there were Megan and Alice and Simon, and over at one of the tables, Marjorie and my father and a few brave souls of their generation, suffering among the young. There was the faithful Rilly, near the edge of the dance floor, her generous bosom making what looked like a bid for freedom from the confines of her bodice, which was two sizes too tight. The rest of The Glass Menagerie was faces: whitish circles bobbing up and down in the semi-darkness. The spotlight was on me. I put out my hand and touched the glass. How strange, I remember thinking. Before I touched the glass, it was as if nothing but clear space surrounded me. I was a bird: an enormous scarlet bird flying high, high above everyone. Now, because I was aware of the invisible walls, I felt imprisoned, crushed, unable to breathe. Greg's words from the very first time I ever sang with the band came back to me. 'You're a trouper, Bella,' he'd said.

'That's what you are. A real trouper.' I blinked tears out of my eyes. Troupers didn't cry. Troupers sang even though ghastly tragedies had happened, were happening in their private lives. Remember Edith Piaf, I told myself. Sing like her. Be as tough as she was. The first few bars of the introduction to 'Get me out' hit me like a blast of fresh air, and I thought: what a good song to start with. That'll get everyone's toes tapping. I began the first verse:

> I'm in a prison
> that you can't see,
> bars of love
> surrounding me.
> Let me out!
> Get me out!
> Take this cage
> away from me.
> My poor old heart
> just wants to be free . . .
> Let me out!
> Get me out!

The last few bars of the first verse reached my ears and sounded very peculiar, as though they'd been stretched and distorted. I kept on singing. I thought I kept on singing, but all the words became jumbled in my mouth, as though they were sticky toffees I'd been sucking, caught around my teeth. I stopped and looked down at the pale discs of faces below me, all of them turned towards me to see what I would do. I remember thinking: I must be very ill. I am seeing things. There's Mark. There, at the edge of the crowd, pushing his way through towards me. I am going to close my eyes, and when I open them, he'll be gone. He is a dream. He is my dearest wish. I remember closing my eyes. I remember nothing but the dark, nothing but falling through miles and into a black lake of silence.

Now, now that it's all over, fragments of what happened next come back to me, like pieces of a jigsaw puzzle that I have to fit together. First, there was a voice, saying, 'Let me through. Let me through. I'm a doctor.'

'But you're not a doctor,' I said to Mark, later.

'No, but I will be,' he answered, 'and I wasn't going to let anyone touch you. No one. Not before I'd reached you.'

'So what did you do?'

'I gave you mouth-to-mouth resuscitation,' he said.

'The kiss of life,' I sighed.

'If you feel like being romantic about it.'

'I always feel like being romantic.'

Mark grinned. 'I'd noticed.'

'You don't seem to mind,' I said.

'I guess I could get used to it,' he said. 'With practice.' Then he kissed me, and another piece of the jigsaw floated into my thoughts: lying there on the floor of the glass cage and seeing very close to my face someone looking at me with eyes the colour of aquamarines. I think I said something silly like, 'What are you doing here?' and he said (I'm sure of this because it struck me as very funny, even then), 'I'm a friend of the Maxtons.' I giggled weakly and said, 'No, I mean, why aren't you in Boston?'

'It's the Christmas vacation,' he said, as though that explained everything.

I have some clearer answers now. Mark has a Scottish grandmother whom he visits every Christmas.

'You will meet her,' he said, 'when we go up there next week.'

'Am I coming with you?' I asked.

'I'm never letting you out of my sight again,' he said.

'That's very high-handed of you. I might have plans of my own.'

'Have you?'

'Yes,' I said.

'Okay,' he sighed. 'Let's hear them.'

'I plan,' I said, 'never to let you out of my sight ever again. I thought I'd lost you.'

Mark smiled. 'Not me. I knew I'd find you.'

'How did you know?'

'I would've turned this dinky little island of yours inside out looking for you, is how.'

'You didn't even know my name.'

'I would have described you to the Maxtons. The Maxtons know *everybody*.'

I started to laugh. 'Everybody who is *anybody*,' I said, and Mark joined in the laughter.

'Stop,' I said. 'I'm out of breath.'

'We'd better practise that kiss-of-life thing again, right?'

'Definitely right,' I breathed, and closed my eyes.

Now, I am sitting in the buffet at King's Cross. Megan and Alice will be here in a moment. So will Mark.

Yesterday, I went to say goodbye to Pete and the band. I took them each a pair of woolly gloves as a Christmas present.

'A different colour for each of you,' I said, 'so that you don't get them mixed up.' I smiled at them, all sitting at the kitchen table in their usual places, each with his own special mug in front of him.

'We wish you luck in Boston, Bella,' said Greg. 'They won't know what's hit them. And you can come back and sing with us any time. We'll miss you.'

'And I'll miss you,' I said. 'All of you.'

I left the house quickly and walked down the dark street without looking back.

I can see Megan and Alice through the window. Soon, they will be waving goodbye to us, to me and Mark, as we leave for Scotland on the overnight train. Tonight, I thought, tonight my happy ending will begin.

THE
TOWER
ROOM
BY
ADÈLE GERAS

'I'm going to kiss you,' he said. 'If you don't mind, that is.' I couldn't speak. I just closed my eyes and waited. He kissed me very softly on the lips, so that I could hardly feel it, but I smelled his smell in my nostrils, and his hands were on my shoulders. I opened my eyes.

Megan, Bella and Alice survey the drama of everyday life from the Tower Room of their isolated boarding school, Egerton Hall. As their schooldays draw to an end they are already sensing the dangerous delights awaiting them in the outside world. But as Megan looks down one unforgettable morning and meets Simon's inquisitive gaze, her safe, cocooned world is soon transformed forever.

The Egerton Hall Trilogy:
The Tower Room ISBN 0099409542 £4.99
Watching the Roses ISBN 0099417235 £4.99
Pictures of the Night ISBN 0099409739 £4.99

WATCHING
THE
ROSES
BY
ADÈLE GERAS

'I don't know if I can tell it properly but it's about an Ill-wishing.'
'You mean a curse?'
'They call it The Ill-wishing in my family,' I said.
'Who's had this malediction put upon them?'
'Me.'

Something is very wrong with Alice – poisoned with dark memories and unable to speak to a single soul, it seems the Ill-wishing placed on her has come true. Even her closest friends don't seems able to save her from the nightmare . . .

Based loosely on the fairytale Sleeping Beauty, this is a haunting tale of treachery and betrayal.

The Egerton Hall Trilogy:
The Tower Room ISBN 0099409542 £4.99
Watching the Roses ISBN 0099417235 £4.99
Pictures of the Night ISBN 0099409739 £4.99

TURNABOUT

Margaret Haddix

You're going to be able to walk again. You're going to be able to see well again. You're going to be able to hear. I don't know about immortality, but I can promise you this: You're all going to be young again.

What would you do if, on your deathbed, you were offered another chance at life? Selected for Project Turnabout, Melly and Anna Beth are given an injection to reverse the ageing process. At first the results are astonishing, but then they discover that the follow-up shot, designed to halt the process, has proved fatal to all who have taken it.

Now teenagers - and growing younger by the day — they need to find someone to take care of them. But whom can they trust?

ISBN 0099427087 £4.99

I Capture the Castle

DODIE SMITH

As they came toward the barn, I heard them talking. Neil said: 'Gosh, Simon, you're lucky to get away with your life.'
'Extraordinary, wasn't it?' said Simon. 'She didn't give that impression at all last night . . . and they obviously haven't a cent. I suppose one can't blame the poor girl.'

This is the journal of Cassandra Mortmain; an extraordinary account of life with her equally extraordinary family. First, there is her eccentric father. Then there is her sister, Rose - beautiful, vain and bored - and her stepmother, Topaz, an artist's model who likes to commune with nature. Finally, there is Stephen, dazzlingly handsome and hopelessly in love with Cassandra.

In the cold and crumbling castle which is their home, Cassandra records events with characteristic honesty, as she tries to come to terms with her own feelings. The result is both marvellously funny and genuinely moving.

'This book has one of the most charismatic narrators I've ever met.'
J.K. Rowling, author of the Harry Potter books

ISBN 0099845008 £5.99

SUZANNE FISHER STAPLES

Shiva's Fire

Parvati looked at her mother. She wanted to live with what she knew was the truth: that dance was as much a part of her as the blood in her veins, the breath in her lungs. She would never have guessed it could cost her the person she loved most.

Even as a baby, Parvati is thought to have supernatural powers, which, as she grows up, seem to spring from beneath her dancing feet. Recognized by the great master of Indian classical dance as a rare talent, Parvati is invited to study with him in Madras and she begins a rigorous training. But then she meets a gentle-eyed boy with his own extraordinary powers. And as he turns her life upside down, Parvati learns that destiny can be an elusive thing.

ISBN 0099409631 £4.99